# THE GODS GIVE MY DONKEY WINGS

JAMES BARR

*To*
*ELIZABETH, EVA, ROBERT ALLAN, RUSSELL,*
*MARIEL GRACE MARGARET,*
*AWFUL LITTLE DONKEYS.*

# CHAPTER 1

Evening was upon the land when I made out the collection of thatched cottages for which I had been in search this many a day. Early in the forenoon I had stopped to allow my weary ass to drink from the brim of a pool at the foot of a fall, and myself to bathe feet in the cool waters. It proved a harsh climb before we reached the plateau across which the river wound its course, but the top once gained I knew myself to be on the verge of a discovery.

Ahead a great mountain pierced the clouds, its mutch of snow drawn tightly around its head and tied under its chin by two ribbon-like glaciers, which, as I guessed, fed the bustling little river along whose bank I now led my patient donkey. The mountain, it seemed to me, looked down upon the valley with considerable good humour, and as I plodded along I could see the deep shadows of evening playing on its gigantic shoulders like the battalions of a mighty army manœuvring for a favourable position. The sun had disappeared by the time I reached the Thorp, but a gentle breeze, blowing up from the plain, tempered the air of the mountain to sweetness with its fragrant balm. By the people I was kindly received. There appeared to be much disputing as to which of them should have the honours, as they were good enough to consider it, of entertaining me, there being no inn or other house of public hospitality in the place. However, the matter was soon settled, for the good people saw that my ass and I were weary, and I was taken in hand by a handsome, strapping, fairfaced young man who led me with many signs of goodwill to a house, wherein I found a woman, she might be some few years older than mine host, and three fairhaired, round-faced children. As I had feared, the good people could not understand me, although I addressed them in many tongues. This was like to prove of some inconvenience to me, a packman, with a healthy itch for gossip.

My pack safely indoors,—be it known a packman's first thoughts are for his stock in trade, then for his ass, and lastly for himself—the grime of travel washed away, I sat me down to an abundant table which the good-wife had prepared for me. About me all was clean to a fault. The floors were polished until I grew suspicious of my red leather slippers, the platters of beaten copper were burnished to the reflective powers of a Christian's mirror, and the table of white wood reflected the light of the taper which burned fitfully by my elbow. I could see that cleanliness was the good woman's god, and as a packman must ever humour the whims of the people, I made a note to have my slippers handy and to remove my shoes at the door, like a heathen worshipper, before entering her house. I think this little thoughtfulness won me the woman's good opinion.

When I had eaten my fill and drunk to my hostess in a good flagon of home brew, my host took me by the hand and led me out into the one street of the place. It was a narrow thoroughfare paved with cobblestones, with on either side a row of houses, each leaning comfortably against its neighbour, their great, overhanging, thatched eaves alive with twittering swallows, and their windows blinking blandly across the way. The people, too, appeared to be hugely sociable, for the men of them sat on wooden benches under the eaves in groups, gossiping and cracking jokes, and swigging great mugs of their brew; and the women stood together with weans of all sizes and ages romping about their knees, talking too and enjoying the cool of the evening. Mine host, with every manifestation of civility, led me down the street, introducing me as I took it, to group after group, who all stood up when I bowed to them, and took off their reed-braid bats to me. They were, as a body, splendid men, the copper of the open air on their cheeks; the clear light of mountain views in their eyes: broad-chested, loose jointed, and frank of face. Honest men there could be no doubt, frugal and sober in their habits, and in their souls a wholesome fear for the gods.

Now as all people well know, a packman is accustomed to take note of the little things that indicate to the thoughtful mind great things; for to him, people, be they merry, or be they sad, fain would present but one aspect of feeling. And if he is to view life with its varying lights and shadows, he must be on the alert to note the small, and reason thence in a logical way until he arrives at the great. And this evening as I walked between the groups of people, I quickly became aware of a sense of unrest pervading the Thorp. The impression soon became strong on my mind that something had disturbed, or threatened to disturb, the quiet of the place. The very goats that frequented the street seemed to have caught the fidgets and continued to lie down, chew their cud for a short time, and get up only to lie down and chew their cud again. That something untoward had happened, or was about to happen, I felt in my bones; but what this something might be was, of course, out of my power to divine. Whether the subdued excitement was of a pleasurable kind or no I could not quite make out from the faces of the people, for the different groups looked upon the matter in wholly different ways. The young men of mine host type seemed to treat whatever the question or matter might be with considerable contempt, as something unworthy of general discussion, and they drank their beer lustily. On the other hand, the old men sat with grave faces and smoked solemnly their long reed pipes, touching but little liquor, and occasionally shaking their hoary heads the one at the other. But it is to the women I turn for anything in the way of palaver. I found that they were discussing the situation with more vehemence than I could have credited, taking into account their cheery faces and buxom proportions. They stood in knots of eight or maybe ten, and all spoke at once at a tremendous rate and then fell into silence, looking at each other with looks which said that truly the strangest things imaginable happen in this world.

We strolled down the street my host and I, and as we

passed along he said a cheerful word here and made a kindly inquiry there; but as we walked I could see that, were it not for the promptings of hospitality, he would long ere this have seated himself to his pipe and mug, to add to the weight of argument his opinions on the question that was causing such a stir. So I took an early opportunity to make him understand that I would, with him, join a group of fellows towards whom he had been casting wistful glances. An expression of pleasure stole into his honest face, and seating me, he brought for me a pipe and a mug of reaming brew, and himself sat down happy. With my face to the mountain I could do nothing but gaze at the marvellous scene. Soft darkness had fallen upon the valley and plain below us, but the sun's rays crawling up the side of the mountain struck the ice cap with a million javelins of candicant light until the ice and snow sparkled and dazzled like a crust of jagged diamonds. The great cap high in the blue dome bristled and scintillated and buzzed with brilliant fires.

At first the men around me spoke but little, as is the wont of Arcadians when a stranger comes into their midst; but seeing me wrapt in the grandeur of the scene spread out before me, they fell into passing jocular remarks and clinking their earthen mugs, and it was not long before the hum of pleasant conversation told me that they were at last feeling at home in my presence. I strained my ear to catch one word at all familiar to me, but recognize one I could not. So I settled myself down to enjoy a smoke and rest after my weary days of travel, and to accustom my ears to the strange tongue. That I would soon pick up the language of the people, I had no doubt.

One skilled in many languages easily acquires an additional tongue.

I had been comfortably seated but a short while, and the strangeness of my company had only time in a degree to wear from the minds of my companions, when a woman, one of a cluster standing near to our table suddenly stretched out her red arm and pointed down the way. Instantly all eyes were turned in the direction, and the next moment a hum of excitement and mutterings ran along either side of the street. The women snatched their children into their arms, and the men discreetly put their huge beakers out of sight under the benches and straightened their backs into a stiffer and more respectful attitude. What in the world could be approaching! In foreign parts, more especially in remote niches among mountains, one never can guess what strange creatures are indigenous. I rapidly glanced in the direction towards which the woman pointed, more than half expecting, if the truth be told, to find some monster of the mountain, some ogre or giant-of-one-eye, with maybe a head or two of his own on his shoulders, a half dozen of other folk's at his girdle, and a great bludgeon in his hand, come swinging down the street. But no! Instead of monster or giant or dragon, all I saw was a group of three marching towards us in the middle of the way; a man and two women, or, to put them in the order in which they traveled, a woman and a man and woman. Certainly nothing here to fear, and nothing to cause excitement. But excitement the pedestrians did cause. So far as I could judge every man, woman, and child watched the progress of the three with a degree of interest curious to note. As they approached, I saw group after group arise from the tables, and first making a deep reverence to the three, remain standing until they had well passed. Although in my soul I abhor bowings and scrapings, there is that in etiquette due to an host which disarms personal likes and dislikes. So I made ready to do as those with whom I found myself were doing.

But in my bowing I took good care not to protract it so long as to miss the chance of taking a calculating view of the three, who, truly there could be little doubt, were of considerable importance in the Thorp. Of the three, I saw at a glance that there was but one of substantial authority; a woman, tall, heavy of bone, with a determined face of hectic hue, a prominent nose slightly hooked, and a reasonable moustache to either side of her upper lip. Her eye was defiantly fiery, she walked abruptly erect, and brought her heel down with a reliant ring on the cobble-stones of the street. A woman from whom may the gods defend me—as from each and all of her class—if I do her not an injustice.

To one side of her, but half a step behind, puffed along a stumpy, little man, a good ten years older than the She if I guessed the truth, a squat body of short legs and a sublime stomach, and a benign, if henpecked, expression; and as he stumped and puffed along, his eyes wandered wistfully to the tables by the way, and to the groups of jolly villagers, and I saw that he knew to a nicety where the flagons of brew were secreted, and I could well believe how he yearned to take his place at one of the tables and crack jokes with the best of his neighbours. But, poor soul! he had become entangled in the skirts of the determined shrew—for shrew I made up my mind she must be,—and was now being swept along at a greater rate than the gods had ever intended his short legs to carry him. To the left of the termagant, also half a step behind, strode a young woman, at a hazard I should say, eight-and-twenty. A glance sufficed to tell that she was the daughter of the termagant. She had the build and looks of her mother, with a certain jejuneness pervading her expression which instantly robbed one of the feelings of awe that instinctively came to the soul at the sight of the shrew. Her fulvous hair had in places broken loose, and her pale blue eyes were watery and indefinite, but her nose was in the air and she wibble-wabbled along, the personification of rigid propriety and paucity of brains. I paid but little heed to her, for I was fascinated by the great woman as she marched her band triumphantly down the street.

We were all so busily engaged in watching the interesting three, that no one of us seemed to have noticed the approach of a fourth person from the opposite direction. Indeed, I believe it must have been the termagant herself who discovered to the spectators the presence of another, for it was plain to us all that a look of hatred and contempt overspread her face, and that she unwittingly paused in her stride at the first sight of the new-comer. And when we followed the direction of her glance, we found a young man moving towards us. He carried over one shoulder a sack half filled with some substance of a dripping nature, and which must have been uncommonly heavy in proportion to its bulk, for the burden gave him a perceptible list to one side as he walked. The thrill of sensation which had run through the people at the appearance of the three was now intensified to an audible murmur, which continued until the three and the young man were about to meet at a point nearly opposite where I stood. Then the murmur ceased, and a startling silence fell upon the people. The young man came swinging along, indifference depicted on his face and in his very gait, no devil-may-care air about him, but the bland unconcern that tells of a spirit careless of the censure or praise of on-lookers, whether it be as to his character, dress, or manner. When he came opposite the three, he pulled off his straw plait headgear to them, out of mechanical politeness I could see, for he did not so much as raise his eyes to one of them. As for the termagant and her brood, they none of them returned his salutation by look, word or action; but after the momentary pause, swept on down the street, the great woman's face more fiery than ever, and the man, poor soul! although that were indeed difficult, looking uneasier than before.

Now a packman knows when he has seen anything of more than ordinary importance, and that this meeting seemed in the eyes of the people an episode of exceptional moment, there could be no room for doubt. I saw that the people were quite unable to take their attention off the pedestrians until the three disappeared in a door at one end of the Thorp, and the one in a door at the other end of it. When this happened, the people gazed in open-mouthed wonderment the one at the other for a space of time, and presently, as if a signal had been given, fell to talking, hammer and tongs. The women rapidly dropped their children to the ground, and while with one hand retaining control of them by the scruff of the neck, they gesticulated frantically with the other; while the men, more phlegmatical by right of sex, lighted their pipes, groped under the seats for their mugs, and took a swig before turning to the discussion of the incident, tragic or comic, whichever it may have been. Certainly the affair aroused my curiosity to a pitch that I there and then made up my mind to bide in the Thorp (given reasonable success in driving my trade) until such time as I had discovered what it was all about. Even a packman has his foibles and my greatest, I fear, is a lively curiosity regarding the affairs of my neighbours, a failing—if it be a failing at all—which prevails in many parts of the globe. I went to bed that night with a feeling that something of interest was in store for me.

## CHAPTER 2

The next morning I arose before the sun, for the air of the morning is the breath of life, and taking my ass, I led her gently along the brink of the stream that flowed by the Thorp, allowing the patient beast to crop the rich grasses that grew by the way, while I speculated on the strange scene of which I had been a witness the evening before, and tried to satisfy myself as to whether the people among whom I so unexpectedly found myself were likely to be shrewd at a bargain, and well informed touching the quality and cost of my wares. It gave promise of a glorious day. A few fleecy clouds swung around the base of the mountain and dragged slowly from point to point, catching at the jagged shoulders of rock as though, like young birds, afraid to launch themselves upon the air, and trailing reluctantly up, and up, and up, increasing in size as they progressed until a number of them, joining their ragged edges, at last adventured against the blue sky of morning. Birds sang cheerily, and the bleating of goats was on the air.

I slowly made my way along a goat-track that followed the winding of the stream, and had reached a point as near as might be to half a Christian mile from the Thorp, when I became aware of a movement in the waters behind me. Quickly glancing over my shoulder—not that I feared, to be sure, but it is as well to be on one's guard in a strange land—I beheld the nose of a canoe coming round the bend not so very far behind me. I wondered who he could be that came abroad thus early, for few but philosophers, who should know better, stir abroad a moment sooner than necessity compels. Choosing a comfortable seat by the side of a huge boulder that hung over the brink of the stream, I resolved to wait the coming of the canoe, and to speculate on the cause of so early a journey. As the craft came nearer, lo! I beheld, flourishing the paddle with enthusiastic vigour, the young man of the previous evening's episode. His head was bare, showing a great clump of tangled hair, his jacket loose, and his chest and arms exposed to the cool morning air, were knotted with muscles that writhed and doubled to the sweep of his paddle as he shot the canoe against the stream, which here flowed rapidly. As he approached me, I took occasion to examine his face with a more minute scrutiny than had been my privilege when first I saw him. It was an open face, shaven, bright and frank, with eyes of piercing clearness, features sharply defined, straight nose, and decided chin. He did not sight me until his craft was almost abreast of the point where I sat; but when at last his eyes fell upon me, he gave no start nor any look of surprise, but called to me in a pleasant, manly voice some words which I took to be a morning greeting. I returned the salute speaking in my own tongue. At this he turned his face quickly towards me, at the same time checking the course of his canoe, and for a moment he ran his eye curiously over me. Gently dipping his paddle into the water to keep the canoe abreast of me, he seemed to hesitate as one searching the dictionary of his mind for a word, and at last replied in the language I myself had used, but with the stilted precision of one unaccustomed to the tongue.

"A glorious morning, indeed."

Now this was a pleasant surprise to me. I had despaired of finding anyone in the Thorp who was at all familiar with my tongue, and one's own tongue from the lips of another is music in a strange land. Continuing, he inquired:

"You are a stranger in these parts, sir!" to which I replied in the affirmative, and in return asked him if he were a native of the Thorp.

Yes, he had been born and had lived his life in the Thorp. He said I would find few in those parts to speak my tongue; and when I told him that, himself alone excepted, in my forty-two days' travel I had met with none who could, he replied that so far as he knew no one understood the language, and be, more's the pity, but imperfectly. How unfortunate that this should be so, for there was one matter only that exercised my curiosity, and of that I could not be so ill-bred as to inquire of one whom I knew to be a principal to the striking incident. This would be more than even a packman's inquisitiveness allowed. But not to be completely beaten, I cudgelled my brains for some way to introduce the subject of last evening's street scene without giving offence. If I failed to get a clue from this young man, who alone of all the people could speak my language, there was little likelihood of my coming to the end of the mystery without a great wrack of brain and speculation, if, indeed, I came by the end at all. So I said:

"I saw you, did I not, walk down the middle of the street last evening?"

He again glanced quickly at me, and a playful smile flitted across his face as he made reply:

"Many people did, if my memory does not play me false."

Now this I took to be a mild rebuff to my inquisitiveness, and as I well know, a man whois over curious cannot afford to draw suspicion upon himself too early in the game, for people, unthoughtful and perverse, as a rule insist on telling the news to those who do not care to bear, and withholding it from those who, like myself, are athirst for even the meanest item. The young man's answer at once made me more cautious. Unfortunately, it did not, on the other hand, assist towards the solution of the mystery. After a pause, and as if to neutralise the slap in the face, he asked me if I would look in at his house at sundown, saying that he would much like to have a chat with me, and I, glad of the opportunity of a crack, answered him that it would give me great pleasure to experience his hospitality. He described to me his house, so that I might have no difficulty in finding it; but I noticed that he did not mention his name, nor did he ask mine. As we were speaking, he had run the nose of his canoe into a patch of white sand, and stood for some minutes arranging a clump of dry rushes that had been dipped in some greasy substance, the whole affair looking very much like a flambeau. This securely fixed in an upright position at the bow of the canoe, my young friend resumed his seat, shoved off the sand bar, and, flourishing good-bye with his paddle, disappeared around a point.

And now I found yet another matter to agitate my curiosity. Where in the name of goodness could the young man be going? Already he was among the roots of the mountain. From where I sat began the upward sweep of the mountain, and every step in the direction in which the young man had gone was a step skyward. Moreover, I could hear the roar of falling waters ahead. Yet the man in the canoe had paddled away as if be were bound for a journey of some duration. This surely was an uncommon thing. But the sun had risen, and mine host might be wondering what had become of me, so back I started, leaving it for a more convenient season to discover the secret of the stream.

That afternoon the man in whose house I found myself so comfortable, by signs and beckonings led me to understand that he wished me to accompany him, but where or why I was, of course, unable to guess. I put on my cap, and taking my staff pointed to my pack and looked inquiringly at him, for it crossed my mind that he had tired of me, and wished to find me other lodgings. But no; he shook his head, and signalling me to leave the pack, we made off. Down the street, some seven houses or so distant from mine host's, we came to one of more pretensions than its neighbours, having above the door of it, and protected from the weather by an alcove of deftly woven willow, three modelled figures in clay, as I guessed, the totem of the Thorp. Without knocking, my guide pulled the latch-string and entered a room which had all the appearances of a waiting-room. In this lobby we found no one, but before we had closed the outer door plainly heard voices in high debate. It was a masculine voice that spoke as we entered, but in a moment this was silenced, and the strident notes of a woman's tongue, cutting short the first speaker, poured forth a raging torrent of words, which in turn was interrupted by a decisively spoken sentence, delivered in a tone which I thought I recognised. The female's tirade was checked but for a moment. The verbose torrent swept away the barrier, and began with renewed fury to rage on its way, and the next instant the door, opening into the room in which we were, flew back upon its hinges, and striding from the inner room came my young man of the canoe, and tripping after him a dainty little lady. My acquaintance held his head proudly in air, but his lips were drawn, his clear eye flashed fire, and one with half an eye could tell that he was angry from the crown of his head to the sole of his foot. His cloak brushed my knees, so closely to me he passed, yet he was so absorbed in whatever had taken place that he did not see me. But the girl certainly did, for she shot a roguish glance from her black eyes, and gave me a smile that was, despite her pluck, quite half a sob-a smile which dimpled her cheeks as she passed us, and without pausing she tripped through the doorway under the arm of the man who held the door open for her, and we were once more alone in the entry. She quite took my breath away did this slender, roguish maiden, and, old bachelor packman that I am, I fell in love with her at first sight, as, indeed, I do with most women who are little and plucky and young. The woman's voice still sounded from the inner room, and to give him his due, I could see that every word she spoke was drunk in by mine host, and doubtlessly stored away for future recapitulation. It may be that a laudable ambition to be in a position to tell a finished tale to his less fortunate townsmen had as much to do with his delay in making our presence known as had a gallant hesitancy to break in upon a scolding wife.

As we stood in the waiting room, I thought of the custom that obtains in Christian lands—I speak of those Christians, for I have but lately returned from a journey to their abodes. Those strange people, then, have a custom of knocking at the outer door and waiting until invited from the inside to enter. To be sure, it is a custom that would never be put up with here, for it assumes on the part of the owner of the house an unreadiness or an unwillingness to receive whosoever asks for admission, neither of which assumptions is creditable to one party or the other. But it occurred to me that in this particular case the Christian practice would be of some convenience at least. However, there was nothing for it but, after listening a reasonable time, to open the door and walk in. This, therefore, we did.

The room into which we stepped was larger than that we had quitted, and furnished in a more becoming fashion. The walls were hung with tapestry, well-modelled figures of clay occupied niches, and the furniture was richly carved and of substantial proportions. But not the furniture, nor the size of the room, nor the tapestry and ornaments attracted my interest. For deeply sunk in a great cushioned chair, his hands thrust well into his pockets, his fat legs stretched before him, and a most woebegone look on his podgy face, sat the old man I had seen on the previous evening hurried down the street; and walking the floor, in a hurricane of passion, the masculine she, the termagant, rage writ on her every feature, who, as we entered, shot one withering glance of contempt at the old man. He appeared to be about to hazard a reply to her ragings when his eye fell upon us, and she, noticing a ripple of recognition pass over his face, looked sharply around. Without acknowledging our salutations, she strode out of the room like an indignant ogress. Whew! Thank you! No lace shall I try to barter with you! The very sight of you has taken my breath away!

The old man glanced timorously over his shoulder to make sure that she had gone, and when he saw that she had indeed quitted the room, he threw his head in the air, as though tossing away the remembrance of her tongue, withdrew his hands from his pockets, and sat up in his chair, a melancholy grin overspreading his countenance. Mine host took me by the hand as if I were a child, although I was old enough to be his father, and, leading me forward, bowed to the old man, and said something of which I could not understand one word. But a packman knows the language of the face, the lips, the eyes, the very wrinkles, and I guessed that I was being made known to a dignitary of the Thorp as a stranger within its gates. Poor fellow! I could well believe that he was a kind, old man, with a great heart that had not yet been sapped of all its juices, or completely crushed under the heel of domestic adversity. He arose and laid his hands impressively upon my head and spoke, a benediction it might have been, so solemnly were the words uttered. He seated us, and when he turned to mine host, and especially after he had brought to us something in the shape of good liquor, I saw with joy the jovial, sociable soul of the old man expand, until presently it beamed from his fat face. We sat with him for a long time. When at last we arose to depart, he saw us to the door, and gazing away to the mountain that, covered with snow, towered to the sky, —snow no whiter than his own hair—he repeated the benediction. As I walked away, I could not but feel a touching sorrow for the old man. And that termagant! The gods protect me, an old bachelor, from her, and from the likes of her! May the spears of the followers of the false prophet Mohamet pierce me; may the cruel after-life fires of the Christians warp me; may the rods of the Confucian fall upon the soles of my feet, and the dread spells of all foreign gods and devils combined be upon my soul, rather than that I should fall into the keeping of a scolding wife! Ah, what a difference to turn the mind from the termagant to the little lady who had tip-toed so gracefully after the young man! And, by the way, what in the world were the two of them, the little lady and the young man of the canoe, doing in the presence of the termagant and the old man? They were exactly the people I did not expect to find together. And why had the termagant flown into such a deplorable rage? "Confound it all," I said to myself, "I must bestir me to learn the language."

In the early evening I took my seat on one of the benches in front of the door where already the men folk, returned from fat fields and pasture lands, were assembling to gossip and to swig, for I determined to hearken attentively to their conversation that my ear might be attuned to their strange tongue. The followers of Christ have it that "to whom the gods hath given, he shall receive the more from the gods;" and verily I believe those strange peoples are not so far wrong as is their wont to be, for I have found with each new tongue acquired an increased ease in acquiring the next. It is but picking a word from this tongue and a word from that, and there one has the language. But first of all, as I have said, the ear takes impatiently to the new arrangement and proportion of sounds, and must be broken in like the foal of an ass. I soon found sitting around me a group of men, sturdy and stoutly built, with thews like supple steel, from much climbing after the he-goats of the mountain, and who drank with a certain grandeur of capacity that charmed me, for truly the world admires a large drinking man as it does a soft spoken woman. The fellows comfortably settled to their benches and their bowls, I could see that the event of last night was still the great subject of speculation, and that mine host had suddenly become a mighty important personage, as compared with the previous evening, was equally apparent. He passed from group to group, followed by an ever-increasing number of listeners eager, as many people are, to bear a second telling of a tale, and in this way he was slowly making down the street. Whatever had happened at the interview this afternoon between the young man of the canoe and the old man of the termagant wife, it was undoubtedly a matter of moment, and a definite step in the career of the dispute. I cannot believe that packman was ever in such a tantalising position as I found myself. The drama acted all around me, and I unable to follow the shiftings of the play. I almost screwed my spirit to a resolve to ask the young man point blank what it was all about, but the thought of the quiet snub of the morning withered the heroic resolution.

Again it occurred to me as I sat there that I might do worse than discuss with myself the question of how the people of the Thorp were likely to look upon my visit to the young man. Undoubtedly he was unpopular. As to that, there could be no question. Would my visit to him include me in his unpopularity? A packman must look sharply to his doings that he mix not himself with the wrong cliques, or his bargain-driving will inevitably suffer in the long run. But when I propounded question and supplied answer I found it came to this : either I must risk a problematical decrease in sales or forego any chance of coming by the truth of the doings which were so exercising my soul. It was a sore choice for a thrifty packman; but I made up my mind to hazard my reputation, and tramp away if I found the people at variance with me. Any packman would have done the same, I feel assured, for gossip is to us as the breath of our nostrils. So I betook me up the street to the house of the young man.

## CHAPTER 3

I pulled the latch-string, the door swung open, and passing at once through the anteroom, I pushed back a heavy curtain and slipped into the house proper, and found—? Myself in the strangest place one could well imagine. A large, oblong room, the floor of earth pounded to a stone-like surface, and smooth, with great blotches of quaintly woven carpets here and there, ceilingless, rafters exposed and the rush-thatch showing through, festooned with many spider webs, and heavy cross-beams hung with strange weapons of the chase and of war. At places, thick curtains of fine material fell toward the floor, and were caught back to make a passage-way, or hung against the wall, and the evening light poured through more windows than I had ever seen in such a small compass. These and many other matters I took in at a glance. But they were trifles in comparison with the chief feature of the great room. For hanging from the crossbeams, swinging from pegs in the wall, lying on the floors, with ghastly mouths open as if in the last throes of strangulation, heaped in the corners, piled up on the floor, grinning, leering, frowning, staring, gasping, crying, laughing, blinking; everywhere, from one end of the room to the other, and up to the ceiling, were strange shapes in clay of the ghastliest white. They filled the room with scowl and smirk, and the place looked the very abode of my youthful nightmares,—my dreams of the after world. The shades of night fitted across the upturned faces, until I began to think I saw several of them wink leeringly at me, and I verily believe that anyone but a packman would have turned tail and fled from the place of awful shapes. Assuredly it was only by a strong effort of will that I screwed myself to the pitch and entered the room. This morning truly I had met with a congenial spirit, for, ah! I love the gods and the makers of them. The fashioner of wet clay, the moulder of grinning faces and strange bodies, the sculptor, the craftsman of the countryside, the soul of art in the body of flesh; in fact, the maker of gods. And there he stood among his gods, a coarse overall about him to keep the clay from his clothes, his bushy head bare, and his cheeks swollen with water which he was about to blow against a dun-clay figure that stood on a pedestal with its wraps of coarse brown cloth at its feet. As I entered, he glanced towards me, but, his mouth full of water, he could only nod a welcome, and continued to blow the spray against the passive figure. This gave me time to look about me. Such gods! Such serviceable gods! Convenient of size, portable, non-interfering, and fashioned for any mood and occasion. To my right, as I entered, stood the god of rain, moulded of a clay which the sun would shiver in an afternoon, so that should the god prove an indolent god, he was so to his own destruction. And to my left there stood, balanced on one foot, the god of the quiet earth, in much requisition in mountainous and volcanic districts where land-slides and tremblings of the earth sorely distress the good folk. The god of the quiet earth balanced on one foot so daintily that should he allow the slightest tremor of the ground, down he himself must come and smash to pieces on the stones arranged around his foot for that very purpose. For the inhabitants of the Thorp, sensible people, looked after their gods, and saw to it that the gods were not only worshipped, but that they did their duty. Among such deities and their brood, water-nymphs, fays, goblins, and strange-horned beasts, I picked my way until I stood beside the man, the creator of clay creatures, the maker of gods.

Some time passed before he even looked towards me, but having wetted the clay figure to a nicety, he proceeded to bandage and wrap it up with strips of damp cloth, fastening these with wooden skewers until the figure stood muffled from foot to head. Not until this was done to his satisfaction did he pause to glance at me—a wistful look it seemed to me. His expression was that of one trying to make up his mind on some point or other as to my friendship, trustworthiness, sagacity, or mental acumen. At last, as though satisfied on the score, he said abruptly enough:

"I am glad you have come. I am going."

I looked him in the face, but said nothing. His brows fell as he continued impatiently in the short sentences of one who is not a thorough master of the language which he finds it necessary to employ.

"I go. I have enough. They stone me in the street. They

point; they jeer. Wait. Their gods shall go done. Who will make them more?"

He ceased speaking as abruptly as he had begun, and bent his gaze upon me, a gaze intended to be of the sternest; but I thought that I could divine somewhere away at the back of his eye a merry twinkle that told of a humorous soul within.

"They will cry aloud to the gods, but the gods will not heed. Drought will fall upon the land. The earth shall tremble to their undoing. For I go. By the gods they shall lose their gods-and more. But you are not as these. You are from afar. Will you do me a service?"

I told him I would be pleased to be of any service to the maker of gods.

"Then you will keep this till the sun rises to-morrow, and when it reaches the height of yonder shoulder,"—he pointed to the mountain,—"you will take it and place it yourself—trust to no one—in the hands of the father."

He gave me a parchment carefully sealed, and addressed with many queer flourishes and figures, but written in the language I understood not.

"The father?"

"The father of the Commune; do you not know him? Have they not shown you to him yet? The white-haired old soul who lives in the house with the Thorp's totem above the door."

"Where you were this afternoon?" I interrupted, to let him know that I had seen him, and of course with a shrewd idea that this might possibly cause him to initiate me into his secret.

"How do you know that?" he asked abruptly. "How

know you I was there? You do not speak the language. They could not have told you!"

"I saw you. I went into the father's house as you came out."

He raised his eyebrows and looked in a very old-fashioned way at me.

"Then you heard?"

"Without understanding."

"Ah, yes! I had forgotten. You will enjoy it all-when you know."

Another sad disappointment.

"I go into the mountain," he continued, in an enthusiastically excited voice. "A league of rock and ice shall cover me from them and their ways. I shall kindle my fire on the shores of the Yellow Lake. The bats shall flutter around me, and the cats of the mountain their flaming eyes will look out of the blackness at me, and I shall mould a god of distorted face, gaunt, and with talons in place of fingers; and when the Thorp cries for a god, I will send one. I go to-night. When I return, I will tell you all."

I followed each word he uttered with attention, for it is only the dull of wit or the inattentive that need ask many questions, or who fail to picture the whole from a small part. I quickly put two and two together. The mountain then was hollow, an extinct volcano with a sulphurous crater, from his mentioning the Yellow Lake, a lake cold and of unfathomable depth, shores of run lava; in fact, a great vault of blackness with a bright circle of light away on high, through which the sun each day would shoot a million shafts of sweetening light into the bowels of the mountain, a fan of brightness that would travel slowly round the lake as the sun proceeded on its course. This strange shore must be reached by some tunnel through the roots of the mountain, worn doubtless by waters that had run for ages. Such a supposition would explain the canoe trip of the morning into the mountain, and the flambeau at the prow to light the craft on its way. A strange place, indeed, for a maker of gods to betake himself to, an inhospitable shore it must be, and cold, gloomy, eerie, and silent. Before a man would exile himself, the necessity surely must be great. Consumed with impatience to know what had caused the estrangement between the village and its craftsman, I was on the point of putting a question to him when he abruptly changed the subject.

"I had a short time at my disposal, to-day." I now report him liberally, "and employed it by making out for you a set of key-words to the language of this Thorp, using your alphabet and giving each word its meaning in your tongue" —here he handed me a scroll—"with this vocabulary you will soon know our language."

After thanking him for his trouble and thoughtfulness, we sat down with flagons at our elbows and pipes in our mouths and fell to talking of the world, and although inquisitiveness gnawed at my heart, I was glad enough to tell him of my travels, for next to hearing gossip, a packman loves himself to gossip. I told him of the Christian lands, and he, growing enthusiastic over his art, avowed that he had a mind to journey thither and show the people what serviceable gods he could make for a reasonable return; and verily, I believe he could do a thriving trade, for they are queer people the Christians, and eternally squabbling among themselves as to which of the innumerable sects of them has the true conception of the attributes, elasticity, energy and power of a God of whom they have not so much as a picture or clay figure. My young friend, on the other hand, could assuredly make them a god about which there would be no shadow of doubt. I told him that they are a rich people, and given to running after new gods. So we sat talking late into the night. When at last I arose to go, the maker of gods also got upon his feet, and donning his cap and heavy outer garments, gathered into his arms a great bundle of things that stood ready-rugs, blankets, cooking implements and such like, some of which, indeed, he asked me to carry for him, and we quitted the house together. Outside, he pulled the door to, carefully pushed the latch-string until it fell inside, and taking a piece of red chalk from his pocket, he drew on a polished panel of the door a large circle and then two heavy lines underneath. This, he informed me, was the sacred sign of privacy which all were in honour bound to heed. With that sign on the door none would molest the place, and none would dare to blot the sign from the door save only him who placed it there. The chalk-marks to his satisfaction, we made our way down to the stream where his canoe, deeply fraught, floated to its moorings, and I saw him disappear with a flourish of his paddle into the deep darkness that hung around the foundations of the mountain.

# CHAPTER 4

When the sun had reached the appointed height, next morning, I, as in duty bound, betook myself to the house of the father, and, now familiar with the custom of the Thorp (on this one particular at least), I pulled the latch-string, and at once ushered myself into the room in which on the previous day I had been so kindly received. I found the father seated in the same chair, but, instead of the woe-begone expression on his face, there was an air of bustle and business which pervaded the very room. Before him on the table were rolls of parchment, and on one or two sheets which lay open I saw columns of figures which I guessed to be the town's accounts. Forgetting for the moment that I could not understand his tongue, or I should rather say that I was supposed not to understand it, although, as a matter of fact, I had studied assiduously the vocabulary that the maker of gods had made for me, the father gave me a dignified and kindly welcome, naming me, I made out, the Stranger Within the Gates. Our salaams ended, I took from my breast the epistle that had been given to my charge, and handed it to the old man. He took it, gazed in wonderment at the address and then at me before nervously breaking the seal and reading the document. I watched him narrowly, and as his eye ran over line after line a look of hopeless consternation came into his chubby face. And when he had finished, the missive slipped from his fingers and fluttered limply to the floor, while the old man clutched the table and gasped for breath. Frightened lest he might be about to have a stroke, or some other dire visitation, I made for his side, crying aloud for assistance as I ran. But before I could lay hands to help him, he recovered a little and motioned me back. The blood that had mounted to his face fell again into its proper channels, leaving him pale and his brow purflewed with beads of perspiration. My cries, however, were not without effect. Before I had well ceased calling for assistance a door flew open, and, bursting upon the scene like an embodied tornado, came the she-Samson, demanding, as I took it, to know the cause of the hubbub. The old man's eyes turned towards her, at first with their accustomed look of helplessness, but gradually kindling into a blaze of fury and indignation, until, overmastering his fears, he jumped upon his feet, and bringing his fist upon the table with a rattle that caused even the Amazon to start, began to pour into her volley after volley of verbal grape and canister. No doubt in the harangue he intimated to her the contents of the letter. But, poor soul! he was poaching on his wife's preserves, and soon began to stammer and halt for words. Confusion gradually settling upon him, he weakened, and finally ceased speaking altogether. The termagant, who had stood for some moments as still as a statue glaring down upon him, a look of utter contempt on her masculine face, presently began in earnest. She stormed and ramped and stamped; she skirled her words out like wind among the rocks, her eyes shot a million javelins of angry light into his soul, she scathed him, blighted him, shrivelled him up, cracked him; she lashed him with scorpions, and scourged him to the bone; her red hands played around his white head like the lightnings around a mountain top until I feared for his life—and mine. The gods protect me! I would fay flake by flake, coat by coat, the ashy balloon of the forest hornet until the honey and the eggs showed yellow in the air, rather than draw down upon my head the anger of this termagant. But my time was to come, and not a word could I understand. Would that my feelings were as numb as my ears were unknowing. She whirled on me abruptly, and demanded to know something-the god of chance alone could tell what it might be. I could do nothing but shake my head at her. Again she demanded, and again I shook my head. I could see the father struggling with himself to summon up courage enough to tell her that I could understand not a word she uttered; but before the desirable pitch had been reached, it was too late to save my skin. A third time she demanded, and the ridiculousness of the situation overcoming my usual restraint, I burst into a broad grin, aggravating enough under the circumstances, I have no doubt. The upshot of the matter was that the termagant flew at me like a spit-fire cat, and the next instant I found myself whirled through two doors, and occupying a most undignified position on top of a rubbish heap in the middle of the street. I glanced up and down to see whether or no anyone had noted my undignified out-coming, and was pleased to find no one looking; pleased indeed, for a packman can ill afford to be made a laughing-stock of, if he is to do a driving trade. Woman! woman is—but with the recollection of that exit fresh in my mind, I cannot trust myself to write of woman. I felt that the house of the father was no place for me, and resolved to get as far away from the abode of the termagant as my legs and good grazing permitted. I will risk most things for a friend, but again show myself to that shrew, I would not for the best friend man ever had.

Hastening to where my ass was tethered (for I longed for the company of one I could trust as a friend), I led the sad-visaged beast away toward the mountain, and while she cropped the rich grass I had ample time to smooth my temper and to turn my thoughts to the scene of my mortification. What a sensation the epistle from the maker of gods had caused! First the father in a fit as near as might be, and then still more strange, stung to such a pitch of daring that he actually fell to rating the termagant. And she! Why should she take the departure of the maker of gods so to heart? Little she cared for gods or men, if I may judge of human nature. Yes! there was more than clay gods behind all this. Mystery on mystery, and it worried me sorely.

Now I had not strayed far in quest of grass for my donkey and silence for myself before I became aware of a strange sound on the air, a sound as of the beating of many pinions, and, look about me as I might, I could not make out the cause of this, nor indeed locate the direction from which it came. The sound loomed and rolled and fluttered on the morning breeze, seeming to come at one moment from the sky, and at the next from the earth, and again from the mountain. That I was not the only one to hear I quickly discovered, for in gazing about me to divine the occasion of the strange mellow rumble, I noted that every goatherd of the mountain and every tiller of the soil, near and afar, stood alert and listening. But not for long. Casting away their implements, and leaving their herds to wander at will, the toilers and herders set out helter-skelter for the Thorp as fast as their legs would carry them. The first who passed near to where I stood, without pausing for a moment in his career, motioned me excitedly to follow, and becoming thoroughly alarmed at the noise and its effects upon the people, I bestrode my donkey, and, gathering up my legs to clear my feet of the ground, flailed the beast into a gallop towards the Thorp. We soon fell in with the mass of the people—men, women, and children—all making in one direction, all madly jostling and elbowing to be first, and shouting to one another as they ran, and a uniform look of blended surprise, curiosity, and foreboding on their faces. The length of the street won, we turned sharply to the left, and behind the houses—a spot I had overlooked in my rambles—we came upon a roofless amphitheatre or circus, paved with stone, and in the centre of this, doing duty as an ambo, a huge circular rock, flat on top, and mounted by steps hewn into its smooth side. Around this ambo were placed thirteen seats of stone. Already a great concourse of people had gathered beside this huge boulder and were waiting, the men with heads bare and the women with children in their arms, and many were shouting to each other, but ineffectually, for the strange sound that had startled me on the mountain now became well-nigh deafening in its intensity. Indeed, it so pervaded the place that some time passed before I discovered that I was standing quite close to the whole cause of the ominous sound. A great drum, or it might better be described as a tank, made of staves and sheepskin, and this suspended from a gallows, by thongs of raw hide, half a man's stature clear of the ground, and at opposite sides of it two men stood, their coats thrown aside, their shirt-sleeves rolled up, and perspiration running down their cheeks and chests, as with monotonous precision of intervals they swung heavy mauls, and brought them crashing against the side of the drum. At every beat of this drum a great black blotch of sound flew out and over the countryside; a muffled, hollow, deafening boom that shuddered on the air, an ominous roll of solemn sound pervading the earth and sky like a shadow for leagues and leagues. It oppressed my soul, this spirit of portentous sound; it worked upon my nerves until I was fain to clap my palms over my ears, and my sober ass, who up to this moment, with enviable unreason had never displayed concern at any of the works of the gods or of men, turned tail and galloped away from me.

As soon as this horrible thunder had worn on me so that I might pay attention to other things than the saving of my eardrums from splitting, I looked about me, and made sure from the manner in which those assembled gazed upon the drum that the beating of it was a most uncommon occurrence. Many of the younger men and women watched the beating of the drum in a way that showed them to be completely ignorant of the operation and its effects. Truly to hear the alarm once would last a man his lifetime. But it was towards the stone that I directed my attention. On the top of it stood the father, his hat off and his grey hair gently rising and falling on the zephyrs, like seaweed in the swell of an ocean. His face bore upon it a grave look, and he stood there as still as the rock itself. Dignified he certainly did appear in his exalted place, and at ease too, probably because the virago was not within touching distance of him. On the thirteen stone seats ranged around this strange pulpit sat the elders—grave, reverend patriarchs each one—with long white beards and striking faces. The booming of the drum continued for a maddening time, so long indeed that I wished I had not been in such a hurry in leaving the mountain; but at last its sable wing ceased to beat the air, although for days after it still beat in the recesses of my brain.

I should tell, before going further with my tale, that in a favourable position for hearing and seeing stood the women in a group, and nearest to the stone I espied the termagant surrounded by a favoured few, while at the very outside my eye quickly singled out the little lady of the raven hair, the wench I had seen with the maker of gods when he so abruptly passed out of the father's house. May the gods give my donkey wings if she did not look a roguish lass, with her rosy lips pursed coquettishly, partly in scorn and partly in laughter, and those black eyes of hers flashing fire in all directions. And when her glance fell on me, the gods bear me witness she broke into a golden smile, and gave me the pleasantest, independent diverting nod of her jet head, the little body, that caused all the people to turn and look at me. Whatever the others were thinking about, or whatever forebodings they entertained, this dainty thing was chiruppy[1] and confident. For of all partisans, a woman is the best. When she espouses a man's cause, he may know he has one supporter who will go to any length, and will stick by him through good report and evil. If he be in the right, and equally sure if he be in the wrong, she is steadfast to the end. Then again she seldom fears, and never despairs. When on more or less unsubstantial ground she takes a side, does it ever cross her buoyant little brain that her claimant can be beaten? Of course it does not. Even when a verdict has been given against him, she knows he will triumph in the long run. Why I have never married a neat little wife is more than I can tell. I have met so many in my time, especially comfortable widows, that—well it may be the explanation is that I have met so many. Looking at the little lady it occurred to me then that maybe she knew a great deal more than most of us about the matter that had caused the gathering. As she stood there tapping the stones with her tiny foot, I saw that although they stood apart from her, not a few of the younger women, and a great many of the younger men, cast kindly glances in her direction. As for myself—but I had better say nothing, for I am such a susceptible old fool of a bachelor.

When it was seen that all the inhabitants of the Thorp were gathered around the ambo, when the last goatherd from the mountain, the tiller of the soil, the driver of the yoked ox, the last he and the last she had arrived and stood expectant, the father arose to tell why they had all been called from their toil. He began slowly, and if I judged aright, his language was terse and simple. That his words were enunciated with great distinctness, I am a witness, for even I, unused to the language, was able to catch a large number of words which appeared in the vocabulary the maker of gods had given me. He spoke but a few sentences before drawing from his breast the letter I had carried to him earlier in the day. The purport of his address (I guessed partly from words I understood, but in a greater degree from the actions and demeanour of the father himself and his listeners) was to the effect that he had dire news for the bailiwick, that a trial lay before them all, and it being a matter which concerned the dignity of the Thorp, he had felt it his duty to place at once the whole facts of the case before the people assembled. That he thought the matter of the gravest, both his looks and the extraordinary action he had taken must bear witness. This said, he read the epistle from the maker of gods, reading sentence by sentence, and pausing frequently to allow every word to sink into the memories of the people. During the first part of the letter the people listened attentively, but at last a sentence roused them to fury. An ominous growl went up, and the auditors looked in consternation at one another. The sentence which excited the resentment closed the epistle, and so that the people should be without a shadow of doubt as to its meaning and import, the father repeated it slowly. I strained my ears as he read, and, strangely enough,—unless, as I have since thought, it was intentional on the part of the maker of gods,—every word of the sentence was full of meaning to me, two only excepted. But those two were the key words, bother take them! The sentence, liberally translated, ran: "I state this as my ultimatum to you and the people of my Thorp: You will give me my—, and I will deliver up to you and the elders your—"

Most aggravating! I pulled the scroll from my breast

and ran my eye carefully down the list of words, but neither of those I sought appeared in the parchment. But I held, with the mental grip of a packman, the two words so that I might discover their meaning at the first opportunity that offered. The first roar of astonishment over, I caught a couple of greybeards near me exchanging a sly wink and nodding their heads as if they rather enjoyed the joke, although not caring to do so openly; and a buxom young wench near me burst into a giggle which she instantly attempted to strangle by clapping her hand over her mouth, a proceeding not altogether successful, for an occasional splutter managed to squeeze a way out between her tightly clenched fingers. I glanced at the group of noble dames who surrounded the termagant. They were gesticulating wildly, while the centre figure stood towering above them all, serene, a look on her face, a set to her figure which seemed to say, "What but such base treatment could we expect from the likes of him!" And the lady of the raven hair? Ah! she stood in the same spot, with the same haughty curl of lips, and the same flashing eye, and the same exquisite contempt for the lot of them.

## CHAPTER 5

The first part of the letter I have said had been received with equanimity. The withdrawal of the maker of gods, and a probability of a short crop of the article did not seem to disturb the people as much as I had thought it would. The last part of the letter caused the hubbub. Hoping to learn the meaning of it all, I touched on the shoulder one of the men who stood near by; one who seemed to see considerable humour in the situation, and repeated the first word whose meaning I could not understand. The good fellow admitted that I pronounced the word correctly, I could see that; but his face and gestures expressed his inability to convey the meaning of the word to my mind. But when I pronounced the second word,—ah yes! he could enlighten me as to its meaning, and grinning broadly he pointed to his breeches. Seeing my look of astonishment and doubt, he proceeded to take the cloth of his nether garment between his finger and thumb to show me that it was really the breeches and not his legs he meant. "You give me my—, and I will give you your breeches!" I repeated to myself, craning my neck for a good survey. The elders looked glum enough in all conscience, but assuredly the maker of gods had not gone off with their breeches, for they were fully clothed. Breeches! it could not be breeches, for clearly it was a matter that concerned both women and men. I asked the man again, and again got the same reply, this time substantiated by one or two who stood about me. There seemed to be no doubt about the matter, although head or tail of the business the gods knew well I could not make. It was a matter to be reasoned out as soon as possible. But my speculations were cut short by one of the patriarchs standing up in his place, and in a terse speech proposing a course of action. His suggestion, whatever it might be, was received with acclamation, and the father being appealed to, and signifying his consent, the concourse broke up to the sound of three beats on the great drum.

I thought the business was done with, for the time at least, but in this I was mistaken. For as if with one accord, the majority of the people set out towards the stream, the patriarch who had spoken leading the way. Now it had been my intention to take my pack and call at the houses of the people to do a little in the way of trade on this afternoon, for already I had idled more time than a packman can well afford, but this gathering upset all idea of trade. The people were much too excited to buy. So I resolved to leave my wares where they were, and follow the crowd. Particular man that I am, and fond of knowing the whole of any matter, the fact that there could be no doubt that I possessed the right word in "breeches," and still was unable to make sense out of the message, plagued me more than I can tell. And what a pother the people were in about those breeches! The bailiwick by the breeches had been set by the ears.

As I brooded on the matter we reached the stream, and here I found a flotilla of canoes ready to start, their bows pointed towards the mountain. There was little of bustle or excitement, but men with expressions of great earnestness were taking positions in the canoes, ready to dip paddle and away when the signal should be given. They took with them no weapons, but this was not surprising for they were many, and the maker of gods but one. Some one had brought a great coat of sheepskin which the patriarch now donned, and made slowly towards the first canoe. Having already experienced their uniform kindness to a stranger, and being invested with a packman's share of audacity, and the delectable flames of curiosity burning within my heart, I wilfully placed myself in the old man's way. As I expected, he paused to address a few courteous words to me, which words, I say it without blushes, I pretended to regard as an invitation, and you may be sure, acting my part well, I thanked him, and before anyone could protest stepped into the canoe. At this the patriarch looked helplessly at me, but at length he gathered his robes about him and took the seat that had been prepared for him, and we were on our way towards the mountain. It was clear that the young man in the mountain had made no attempt to keep his hiding-place a secret, for not a moment had been spent in search or speculation, and already we were headed in his direction. This seemed inexplicable to me, for the force now afloat was large enough to overcome the strongest man, and my young artist must soon be laid by the heels and brought back to the Thorp.

When we reached the rock by which I had sat on the previous morning and spoken to the maker of gods, one of the paddlers passed to me a goatskin rug, at the same time motioning me to put it over my shoulders. The bowman had on our upward journey fastened a huge flambeau to the prow of the canoe, and he now set it alight, a great liquid light it made, spluttering and splashing sops of flame into the bottom of the canoe at each gust of the mountain air. Once round the sharp bend we saw the mountain rise before us into the clouds, like a giant bursting through the earth's crust, and ten canoe-lengths ahead yawned a great cavern, black, mysterious, and over the lip of it the waters ran lapping and oily. Now running water, unless it be quite in the open, is a horror to me. More especially is this so in the dark. The lap of water about submerged timbers, the trickle of it under a floor, the swirl of it as it shoots the arches of a bridge, sets my flesh crawling, while all the time exercising a fearsome fascination for me,—the fascination of a serpent's eye for a bird. In all conscience, here was the very thing to fill me with dread. The water ran with ominous swirls out of the mouth of the cavern, the jagged rocks looked for all the world like gigantic moulders and grinders, and from the black throat of the mountain issued a sullen rumble like to the growl of a hungry ogre. To tell the truth—(a luxury in trade, but not so rarely met with outside of business)—to tell the truth, I began to repent of my coming, and to wish I had not been quite so forward in forcing myself into the canoe. But it was clearly too late to turn back, for in we drove, our flambeau, which outside had seemed to languish, now bursting into brilliant flame, and flashing its light against quaintly-shaped rocks and sullen black waters. Herculean pillars stood waist-deep in the water, and balanced on their heads the mountain of rock and earth and everlasting snows; arches of rock sprung from all sides of us in ranks so lofty that the vertexes were lost in darkness; from on high round drops of water, ice-cold and heavy, fell upon our heads or struck the stream on which we floated with a metallic spat. Huge bats, and thousands of them, fretful of the light, flapped about us like witches in a gale and fanned our cheeks with their wings; and, it might have been that my nerves were overwrought, I saw, or thought I saw, which is quite as gruesome, a score of slimy monsters wallowing near our canoe, rising and falling with the run of the stream. These may have been born of a fevered imagination; I would not like to deny that such was the case. But that of which there could be no question, for it dominated the whole place, was the muffled roar that I had heard even before entering the jaws of the mountain.

Here, inside, the rumbling growl made the very waters to heave, and the air to pant, and the foundations of the mountain to rock. It affected me, I imagine, much as if I were cooped inside the great drum while the Thorp-men smote with their mauls. For the second time this day my nerves were being smitten with sounds, and as we slowly proceeded among the sunken rocks, I soon found my brain in such a shattered state that I grasped the side of the canoe with both hands and cried aloud, I felt sure, although I heard no sound come from my lips. After a time I found myself looking at the dark waters, and thinking what a relief it would be to slip over the side of the canoe, and under the palpitating stream to enjoy the silence that might be found away in its depths, and to escape the demon that roared from the cavern. Indeed, I began to fidget and to stare about me for an opportunity to take the plunge; but, fortunately, before my fears quite overpowered me, the explanation of the commotion was forthcoming. It was simple enough, and natural too; and if I had not been stupid from my morning's excitement, I might have guessed it even at the ingate of the cavern.

Our men had for some time been paddling with long, strong sweeps, for here the water ran braided and fast, carrying on its breast hosts of dancing bubbles, which caught from our flambeau many lights, and burned fairy fires to our honour as they passed. Towards a narrow gap we headed, the perspiration running down the paddlers' faces, and the canoe shuddering inch by inch against the foaming flood, creeping and trembling as though itself in fear of the horrible roar, and after an anxious time it nosed between the rocks, and the bowman, grasping a jagged point, with a grand pull swept us through. My jaw fell in astonishment. For I found myself in a cathedral-like cavity of virgin rock, fluted in places after the manner of an organ, and so high that the light from our fambeau failed to show us the roof. Around us all was black, except only in one part of the cavity. Over against our entrance-place I saw a marvellous sight. A great curtain of snowy white fell out of the upper vastness, and beat the water into a billow of foam; a waterfall from the everlasting snows above, it was, which fell through a crevice in the shoulder of the mountain, fell, it must have been, a half a league in its course, carded to the whiteness of wool by the jagged teeth of rock, and waters smote upon waters with the sound of rolling thunder. The cavern was a great sound-board, the home of thunders. Truly, in all my wanderings, never had I seen such an awe-inspiring sight; in lands distant or near to hand, nothing so weirdly awful as this laboratory of the hoarse voice of waters. The spluttering torch in the blackness, the white head of the elder, the reeking oarsmen, the resounding walls, the great bank of dazzling whiteness, the maddening sound of many waters, these formed a picture so quaintly frightful that I could do nothing but grasp the sides of the craft and squeeze until the blood started from my fingertips, which I discovered to my sorrow later in the day.

Our canoe slowly skirted the cavern wall, keeping as far from the foot of the fall as feasible, for there the water seethed and boiled and swirled in a dangerous way, whereas it swung sullen and silent around the walls. The boatmen exercised the greatest caution in this part of the journey; and I noticed that they were making for an aperture in the wall, which opened as nearly as might be directly opposite to our entrance-gash. This reached,—we were too near to the falling waters to please me, I know,—the man in the prow motioned to me to bow my head, for the aperture was so small, and the rocks so closely overhung the water, that I realised it would be impossible for us to enter except we doubled our heads to our knees. I had just done so, and we were prepared to shoot out of this horrible cavern, when the sudden stopping of the canoe caused us all to straighten our backs again. There we saw the bowman on his knees, with one hand held up in a position of warning, while with the other he had grasped a jag of the rock, and so prevented the canoe from entering the aperture. In this position he peered into the darkness ahead, as though to make sure that his eyes were not playing him false, until the patriarch touched him inquiringly on the shoulder. Then he turned, his eyes starting from his head, and pointing into the black hole, shouted a short statement into the ears of the old man. At this the canoe was whirled around until it lay broad-side to the opening, and the torch held in position for the patriarch himself to make an examination. I saw him look for a brief space of time, then jerk his head so suddenly that the back of it came as near as possible to catching me on the nose, for I had been peering over his shoulder in my anxiety to learn what had startled the bowman. The patriarch's eye, though old, had yet the keen vision of the mountain eagle, and had sighted the object before my eyes had become accustomed to the place. The canoe still retaining its position, I again gazed into the hole, and this time got an eerie fright. For there, at my very nose, a horrible grin on its distorted features, its one eye sparkling, and its two rows of ragged teeth gleaming in the light, hung a gigantic cast of the face of the god of disaster. The reason I had not seen it at a glance was that I had trained my eye to look far ahead, little thinking that the object was so near at hand. When the paddlers sighted this horrible face they began to back our canoe away, but again the bowman motioned the men this time to hold their paddles, and, the canoe steady, he stood erect, picked something from a point of a rock, and at once passed it to the patriarch. It proved to be a parchment, which, holding it so that the capricious light fell upon the writing, the old man proceeded to read, first to himself, and then, as I took it aloud, although not a word could I hear for the thunder of the waters. But bear or not, I made a shrewd guess at the contents. My maker of gods knew well with whom he had to deal. Superstition would suit his purpose better than force or flight, for superstition costs nothing, and breaks no bones. He, the holder of their secrets, the moulder of their gods, the receptacle of all their legends and credulities, had turned this knowledge to account to prevent the coming at him of the expedition, which otherwise he would have had to defeat by force. There hung the hideous face of the god of disaster. Behind it, I had little doubt, swung the black countenance of death.

The parchment message was quickly passed from canoe to canoe, and caused a great commotion, I could see. One or two inquisitive crews steered their crafts towards the opening to satisfy themselves that matters were as reported, which verily they seemed to do to their taste, for they paddled away much faster than they had made for the spot. The crafts floated in a huddle like frightened waterfowl; and when the patriarch gave the signal to return, relief was evident in every face. Now having come thus far and braved the frights and dangers of the subterranean passage, I felt annoyed that the old fellow allowed his superstitions to turn him back. I had by this time become accustomed to the sounds and the darkness, and would have given an ell of my finest lace to gaze upon the Yellow Lake and the hollow mountain with its tea-pot lid of sky. The crafty young rascal! He had put his gods to alien uses. But it is thus all the world over. I have seen it time and time again. Those who make gods, or minister to gods; whose especial duty it is, as it is their profession, to serve the gods, they and theirs are the first to put to base uses those same gods which it is their life's work to exalt. The Christians, who have a wonderful assortment of pertinent saws to suit all sides of any question, have one to the effect that familiarity procreates vilipendency[1], and verily I believe those peculiar people in this. Even the gods are not safe. But the most trivial god I have found, if put to an indignity, has an uncomfortable way of showing his resentment, and my young friend must have regretted that he hung this god of disaster all alone in the blackness above the sullen waters that flowed from the Yellow Lake to join the floods from the sky. For the gods have nothing else to do but to remember, and to avenge. Approbation of praise and resentment of slight make up their little lives, and a man who has many things to think of should be careful not to draw upon himself their wrath. The gods have much time on their hands. I thought of this many times in the tragic days that followed.

## CHAPTER 6

Long before we reached the Thorp the people met us, coming at a great rate along the goat-path bordering the stream, and shouting to us as we came in sight. The news spread rapidly; and when I passed along the street to the house of my kind host,—for I was wet to the skin and shivering with cold,—I found in front of every house the little drab god of sorrow, hands to face and hair hanging dishevelled, and the goats home from the mountain gingerly threaded their way between the clay figures. By the time I had made the necessary change of garments, and had taken a good swig of the mulled brew which the kind hostess had prepared for me,—schooled in the way of women, I had taken occasion to place upon her head a cap, a cheap thing but jaunty, and it made the goodwife wondrously kind,—I took my place on the bench to watch the evening sun set fire to the ice and snow on the mountain. As I gazed at the towering height, I could not but think of the enormous mass of earth and ice and rock, full of roaring waters, sullen lakes, bats and blackness, and away inside the little spark of animated clay, the puny head-strong thing called man, who, wrapping his petty dignities, troubles, joys, and hopes about him, had hurried under the immortal hills to spite his fellow gnats. And they, angry little gnats, how they had bravely buzzed after him until they had come upon a bit of clay moulded somewhat after their own image, somewhat after the shape that had been most familiar to them since their eyes first learned to know the smiles of their mothers, and knowing the shape and substance of it they allowed it to frighten them out of their common sense. They had fled, frightened at a daub of clay. The quarrel, I realised, lay between mind and matter, and the mind was in the mountain.

Thinking on small things, my thoughts naturally enough turned to the little lady with the clear eyes and black hair who had given me such a roguish nod of recognition in the morning. She was chirp enough and laughing before the people, would her buoyancy continue in the privacy of her own house? Would not the knowledge that her sweetheart,—for sweetheart I had no doubt he must be, —that he was alone in the mountain, cause her woman soul to fear and make miserable her little heart? Maybe at this very moment her hands were covering those sparkling eyes of hers, and the tears trickling through. The thought made me uncomfortable, and after fidgeting about for a time and trying to settle myself to my brew, I gave the job up as a bad one, and resolved to walk over to the house in which she lived,—I had not gone through the Thorp with my eyes shut,—and see what was happening to her. So taking a bit of lace in my pocket,—for young wenches are fond of lace,—I made my way across the street, and pulling the latch-string stepped into the entry. Now it is a ticklish thing this walking unannounced into the abode of a pretty lass who lives alone, and having reached the age when a man can bide his time, and can afford to show some consideration to the woman-folk, which no fiery young spark will do, I stood in the outer room for a spell of time long enough to allow the lass to give her dress a bit pull here and a ruffle and a shake there, and to cast one glance at her neck-gear, of which maidens in all climes I know right well are more than ordinary suspicious. I was confident the grace thus given her could not have been ill received, for I heard her dainty feet running nimbly about putting things to rights. When the footsteps ceased, I entered and found her sitting there demurely composed—well the gods fly away with my donkey if I could do anything but admire the art of the lady. The wench sat before a tapestry assiduously plying her needle at a border, and she looked over her shoulder at me as though she had only just heard me enter. Her black hair was coiled loosely, and the end of the strand stuck coquettishly over her ear in quite a ridiculous way. Her kerchief was knotted about her neck, and the great apron she wore fitted her like a charm. When she looked at me her eyes sparkled with the liquid brilliancy of diamonds, and her cheeks were aglow with rosy colour, for it is invariably the black-haired witch that has the brightest cheeks. She arose as I entered, and curtsied, a sedate, tricky little genuflection, addressing me in a gentle tone, although mind you, as like as not it was some impudent remark she made to me, for I will not trust a woman who is aware that one does not know what she is saying-or worse still, doing. But, in charity, giving her credit for the best, I returned a greeting in my own tongue, and drawing up a stool I sat down opposite her. There was a twinkle in her eye as she turned to and began plying the needle, and in a little while her under lip began to tremble out of very devilment I know; I could see that at times her sides shook under the merriment which she was trying to keep from bursting out upon her lips. To be sure, the situation was a whit comical. I could not speak to her nor she to me, but the little minx should not have been thinking of that. She, there in comfort, tittering and bright, and her lover buried in the heart of a mountain, in dankness, dreariness, and maybe dismay, making his bed among the lava of an ancient volcano. Had I been a maiden with such a strapping lad courting me, egad I'd have been in a state. But I aver as I sat there looking at her and speculating as only an honest packman can, she, the body, threw her dainty white hands into the air and burst into a peal of laughter, so long continued that, although I was laughing myself, I began to fear for the safety of her ribs. And she had no sooner dried her eyes and taken one squint at me than the fit was upon her again, and she clasped her hands over her face and rocked herself in the chair forward and back, while I sat there with my palms one clapped on top of each knee, and like the old fool that I am, I joined with her till my lungs were sore. It was some time before we came to our senses, and then the witch seemed concerned lest I should take my welcome as being inhospitable, and she brought me as fine a reaming swig as I ever clapped lips to. Faith, she knew good liquor, which is not a virtue a man of experience expects of a woman. The god of the contraries created woman, and has looked after her ever since. There sat I and drank the brew and smacked my lips, and watched the lass; but for the life of me I could not discern the smallest trace of distress in her face, nor where it is still more likely to discover itself, in her movements, for woman can keep a cheery face when her heart is the sorest, and even when hope is gone. No, the little lady was merry enough, and yet I could not believe she had a callous heart. Maybe it was her bravery, or maybe she knew something that others did not; for instance that the maker of gods had prepared a comfortable home for himself on the shores of the silent lake; that he had made many journeys to the spot, taking with him on each occasion necessities and even comforts. So I took the bit lace from my pocket, a pretty pattern it was that had been given me to induce me to buy, and so cost me nothing but the carrying, and presenting it to the lass took my departure when the joy was upon her. It is the way I have to ensure a warm welcome when I again return. My curiosity was increased rather than allayed by the visit. All that I knew definitely was that the father had something that the maker of gods coveted, and *vice versa*; that the expedition against the young man had failed; that the Thorp was in a hubbub, and the young man's lass was cock-a-hoop. Not enough this to satisfy a packman.

Next morning after I had broken my fast, my host beckoned me to come with him, and issuing forth into the open air we made our way towards the house of the father. Reaching this, we found a crowd of men and women surrounding the doorsteps expectantly waiting, and among other familiar faces, and standing well apart as was her habit, I saw my little lady of the raven locks. We had not long been in our positions before the door of the house opened, and forth stepped the father, surrounded by his thirteen councillors. The father held in his hand a scroll, and this he proceeded to read to the assemblage. Having thoroughly mastered my vocabulary, I caught the drift of the document to be a demand for the instant return to the confines of the Thorp of the maker of gods, ending with a dignified threat of future pains and penalties should the sulky craftsman not comply with the strong request. Those around me seemed to look upon it as a weighty document, but little the people know about the working of the brain of one whose days are spent in creating the beauties of life. When the father had done with his reading, the parchment was placed with great care inside a round gourd-like box, painted a brilliant red, and tightly bound with wire, and this was handed to my host, who again beckoning me to follow, made off towards the mountain. I asked him whither he was bound, and making out from words and signs that he intended to journey round the base of the mountain, I went to where my ass was tethered, and, mounting the drab brute,—for my host swung a strapping stride,—I so accompanied him. It was a weary journey on the ambling beast, picking our way among rocks and dangerous goat-paths; but at last when we had made as near as I could judge an eighth of the circumference of the extinct volcano, we came to a brawling mountain-stream that poured down from the snows. This I found fell through a fissure in the rock. Stopping here, my guide took the box in his hand and dropped it into the aperture, and by pointing out the hole and then towards the centre of the mountain, led me understand that the message would float to the Yellow Lake, on the shores of which the truant was encamped, and that its glaring red tints in the dark waters were to attract the young man's eyes. I afterwards found that the people had stretched a net across the stream at a point near to the Thorp, so that no message which the maker of gods might return could float down the stream unnoticed.

Sure enough on the following morning a message from the man in the mountain had arrived, and was found caught in the meshes of the net. There was no mistaking the tenor of the message. When the father read it to the people it turned out to be resolute and defiant. Workmen had been all the morning busily engaged in erecting the framework of something that looked to be a triumphal arch, and these, when they heard the contents of the missive, appealed to the father to say whether or no they were to proceed with their work. After a consultation with his elders, the father told them to go on, and they returned with the unwillingness that men display when they fear their labours will be in vain. Surely they were not erecting an arch to celebrate the return of their craftsman! That would be absurd! It would be nothing more than an encouragement to him to again take the huff, and retire into the earth. Yet I could come by no other explanation, cudgel my brains as I might ; and although sorely put to it, I refrained from appearing too inquisitive, for people despise an inquisitive guest.

## CHAPTER 7

Three days passed, and again the black sounds of the drum vibrated through the Thorp and across the plain. Each day a message had been sent to the truant, and each morning a reply had been found caught in the net, and the replies had grown rapidly sharper and shorter. This time I was fortunate in obtaining a favourable position to see and to hear. The father was agitated. His pride had been touched. His authority had been mocked, and honour of the Thorp placed in jeopardy. When the people were all assembled-for it was compulsory to answer to the sound of the great drum-the father addressed a few words to them, telling them-the meaning was transmitted to me partly by pantomime-that the matter now rested in their hands, for all he had power to do had been done. Then he read the latest from the mountain. My young friend wrote scornfully. He told the father and the Thorp to do their worst,—some stupid thing it would be he had no doubt,—but to go ahead with whatever stupid thing it might happen to be. That their worst was of little account he knew, for he said (conceited young rascal) that there was not an ounce of masculine brain in the whole place when he was absent. He reminded them all that the Thorp would have been known only to the goats were it not for his work-and another's; that they were the flesh and he-and another—the soul; and that although the flesh, like a stubborn ass, sometimes revolted, such a revolt never put the soul to serious inconvenience, and never certainly did the flesh get the better of the soul in the long run. He ended with a scathing sentence to the effect that the father had always considered himself of some importance; but that when he, the father, had to receive his august guest breechesless, he would learn that the man was of no importance, and the clothes all important.

The old man's face grew crimson as he read, and when he came to the end of the letter, and read the last line, "A pretty looking father of the Thorp you will look with bare shanks," I began to think that I would at last have an opportunity to prove the efficiency of certain compounds of herbs and minerals which I had been trying to dispose of —at a shrewd profit, although that could not be known— to the people, but without success, for they persisted in shaking their heads at the lotions and salves, and disbelieving. However, it was not to be, for the old man pulled himself together and stood with his short arms folded across his drum-like breast waiting the people's pleasure. This letter could be looked upon as nothing else than a bad slap-in-the-face for the Thorp. Not one individual in a score of scores will put up with nonenticity[1], and much less will elders of men, with a community at their back to bear the burden of satisfying outraged dignity, put up with slight or slur on the town's good name. From the Thorp's point of view this instance of contempt was made all the more glaring by the knowledge that, as far as I was able to understand, an irresponsible and unimportant person had in his keeping the honour of the place. Now it is well known that those holding temporary authority cannot for a moment admit that anyone not having a gilded chain around his neck and a fur-tipped cloak about his shoulders, can be of more than incidental use to the community. This is so the world over, and yet poets, painters, pundits, preachers, and play-actors, with a self-conceit which the world refuses to honour, have been known to hold that their callings are as high as are those of money-lenders, the dealer in slaves, the publican, and such-like pillars of a country's edifice, whom the people invariably choose to bear the dignities of civic office. And here I had stumbled on a strong example of artistic perversity. A mere maker of people's gods, a carver of rich ornaments which the elders themselves bought of him, this man flouting the very men who supported him; and moreover, if the truth were known, men who had laid past more goods in a twelve month than the maker of gods was likely to treasure up in a life-time. The thing was preposterous. The thing was absurd. Yet the young man in the mountain coolly asked the elders and the people what they were going to do about the matter, and, on my soul, I could see the authorities were somewhat out of their depth. A crisis like this did not arise every day, and I suppose there was no precedent to go upon. If they had been fighting any other body, the elders would doubtless have requested the maker of gods to appear before them, and would have considered that they were conferring an honour on him by allowing him to get them out of their difficulty. But nature built the walls, and superstition flooded the moat that encircled this artist from his adversaries.

After the reading of the letter there followed a grave council. Patriarch after patriarch addressed the assemblage, slowly, solemnly, stately, but without propounding a satisfactory way out of the difficulty. They got no nearer to the centre of the ancient volcano from whence the headstrong artist persisted in firing verbal bombs into the midst of the Thorp. The greybeards prosed away, and the people, having been led to expect a decided course of action, began to realise the seriousness of the situation, and to grumble and murmur at the unreadiness of their representatives to throttle the revolt of their eccentric townsman without further delay. A half a score of the elders having spoken, there fell a long silence. The people were dispirited, and the father and his council looked helpless.

But a flash came from the blue. The termagant, who had stood near to the ambo, her hard features set harder than usual, suddenly hustled an elder from his seat, and stepping into his place began without so much as a preliminary cough to address the gathering. Before she had spoken a half score sentences the words began to pour from her in a torrent. Her clenched fist shook under the very noses of the elders, and she heaped scorn upon their grey heads for their unreadiness; her face grew red as the breast of the firebird, her arms jerked spasmodically, her voice rose to a shriek, and she fairly carried the people off their feet with her eloquence. I saw the father's soul curl up within him when her burning glance fell upon him. She would have no young, shiftless, long-haired dabbler-in-clay flout the Thorp, were she, instead of an old maunderer, head of the council, that she wouldn't! He snap his fingers at them indeed! Why he depended on them for his very bread and brew. Their stock of gods was quite enough for the time being ; but that aside, if she had to tuck up her petticoats, and with bared leg tread the clay and herself fashion the gods to the best of her ability, she must do so rather than let a menial dictate to his superiors. She would show him! He was a thief, for had he not run off with their breeches? Energetic action was needed, and energetic action they would have. Let them, the people, follow her, leaving the members of the council to look wisely the one at the other, and she would show them how to make the young nincompoop sue for forgiveness and mercy; and saying this she jumped to the ground and made through the crowd, her Amazonic face looking for all the world like a Buddhist idol, and the people, carried away by her fury, and catching from her the insanity of rage, closed around her and swept up the street leaving the father seated in the midst of his ring of councillors. Poor man! authority only runs so far as one has power to exercise it, and in this instance it did not run to his wife.

The scene now became a bustling one. Men, women, and children followed pell-mell after the termagant, eager to know what her plan of action might be, and many of them no doubt eager also to resent the insult to the Thorp.

I have found even in countries of the true faith not to speak of savage and cunning peoples like the Christians and Mahometans, that folk are ever ready to turn their hand against any of their fellows who live a life untrammelled by the petty customs and respectabilities that happen to obtain in the land. Those who have only respectability to recommend them cannot brook anything but a like respectability in others. So the people followed like sleuth hounds in fine fettle. The termagant made straight for the stream, and striding along the goat-path that skirted the bank came at last to the great rock against which I had leaned my back on the morning of my interview with the maker of gods. At this point, as I have already told, the river narrowed to a mere gash in the rock, and the boulder hung invitingly over the very edge of the gash. In an instant the crowd divined her purpose, and with a hurrah the men were beside the boulder, and using their united strength began to rock the rock. Farther and farther it swung as their strength delivered at proper intervals told on its balance, until at last, it hung for a moment as though fearing the leap, then slipped a hand's-breadth and plunged with the report of thunder into the deep running waters. As far as I am concerned, I was drenched by the sheet of water the great rock sent flying to the sky, and through the falling spray I saw the termagant, a glorious look of satisfied revenge on her face, and her finger still pointing to the bed of the stream.

It is one thing to dictate terms to an opponent so long as a man knows that whenever it may suit his convenience he has it in his power to say to his enemy, "Very well. You refuse to concede my conditions, so I withdraw my demands for the time being, and we will now resume our normal relations." But to attempt to dictate terms when the enemy holds the key to the position is a very different matter, indeed. In a few hours' time, the chances were, before he ever dreamed of such a thing happening, the maker of gods was likely to find his circumstances changed from the first to the unenviable second of these positions. The water journeying out of the mouth of the cavern struck with a roar the great stone, paused as though surprised at the obstacle encountered, madly ranged around for a time in swirl and eddy, and finding no outlet, ran in spasmodic, angry waves back again into the darkness as if to carry the bad news to the waters above that their ancient bedway had been dammed. The boulder stood quite twice the height of a man above the bosom of the stream, and it so nearly filled the chasm that the waters found a passage only in chinks and caverns, through which it spurted with the force of a syphon. As the stream rose inch by inch, I thought of the grinning gods away in the dark passage, hangingat best only a few inches above the surface of the water. They must be submerged by this time, and the apertures through which we had so painfully crept by doubling our backs until our noses nearly touched our ankles, must now be full of water. The termagant knew what she was about when she led the people to the rock. The man in the mountain, instead of isolating himself from the people of the Thorp, was now their captive. Such a simple way too of turning the tables, but great inventions are usually simple ones. It occurred to me that when the time came for removing this obstruction the matter might prove rather more difficult than had been the placing of it in its present position; but I little dreamt that it would turn out to be an impossibility, and that the falls, which soon began to thunder over the great stone, should stand to this day a monument to the man who went into the mountain.

# CHAPTER 8

It is strange how sayings heard in the earliest morning of one's life will recur to the memory in the most unlikely place, yet at the most opportune moment. As I sat on the brink of the stream watching the waters rise against the boulder, an old saw that used constantly to arise to the lips of the maternal grandmother of my first sweet-heart-before I had yet left my mother's knee-came into my grey head. She used to say, when in the mood to belittle anyone or thing, which old people are given to, that the man who was wetted by the first drops of a waterfall was never known to be drowned. The truth of this saying has long been apparent to me, for truly the waterfalls began before man came to earth. But here, strange to say, I had the opportunity to insure against the death of which I have had many a premonition, a death that I dread. Not that I am given to fear or superstition, but it is better to be on the safe side when it costs nothing. So the people having all followed the termagant to the Thorp again, I got me down behind the boulder and waited until the sun had leaped the head of the mountain, when slopping over the top of the boulder came the first splutter of water, and the gods are good, it fell upon my head—at least, if not the very first drops, still among the first, which is near enough, I daresay. When I made sure of the water on my head, I grasped my stick and scrambled up the bank in time to see a thin glass-coloured sheet lip over the rock and splash upon the pebbles at the foot, washing them into tiny dunes and ridges, dainty bill and dale, for water nymphs to wander amongst. The sunlight glanced on the waters and gilded the pebbly bed of the stream and the moistened streaks of coloured rocks on the side, and quite forgetful that my ass stood in the middle of the street, bridled and with the pack on his back, I sat and watched the birth of the falls, the falls of the man in the mountain.

To my senses at last, and off I made for the Thorp as fast as stiff legs would carry me, hoping to find my cuddy and pack still safe, although I had been absent for more than half the day; but as I plodded on, my thoughts, which should have been for my pack and beast, again turned to the little lady of the raven locks. Had she heard what the people had done? Bad news has never a blistered heel. Poor, light-hearted little lady! her singing would be hushed and her laughter turned to tears when she knew that her lover was now hopelessly cut off from her, and, galling thought to a proud lass, that before he could again kiss her white brow, he must humble himself to those whom he and she despised. It would go hard with her as it would with him.

The man born with the true spirit of barter in him, the

knocks that are given his pride bounce off as though he were made of indiarubber; but to those strange bodies who spend their short lives in scribbling the song and story of the countryside, or streaking the wet clay into curious shapes, or chiselling quaint pictures upon the face of the rock that overlooks the dwelling-places of men, to humble such before the people is to bruise their hearts between two stones. And a woman who sees her loved one tortured thus, she suffers all the pangs—ay, and multiplied an hundred times over. Poor little woman! How the fire would flash from her tear-wet eyes! How scornfully her lip would curl! What disdain would show in the very poise of her pretty head! There were many against her one, and yet he had compelled them to resort to force. The ox in the valley could have done what the people of the Thorp had done. And the last drop of bitterness was added to the cup by it being one of her own sex, the she-dragon, indeed, who had hit upon the way to imprison her lover, and had led the people to the rock. Poor lass! After seeing to my beast, and running over my wares to make sure that no one had made away with anything during the time I was sitting by the side of the stream, I just gave my face a bit rub, and saw to the brushing of my clothes where the clay of the stream had touched them, and after putting a hint of sweet-smelling oil on my hair, I took my staff in hand, and made away down the street to see if I could be of any comfort to the little body. I waited a mannerly time in the entry, and then made my way into her room. She sat at her spinning-wheel, the purr of it sounding in a cheerful snore, and the wheel whirling so fast that it looked for all the world as if it were a whiff of grey cloud, and the little body glanced over her shoulder at me as I entered—a favourite effect of hers I saw clearly. Blithe as a bird, as I'm a living man, her eyes dancing with roguish light, a smile of welcome on her pretty lips, and her pink fingers buried in the carded wood, her black hair, in strong contrast to the fleece, rippling down her back, and her pretty foot curtseying and nodding to the treadle of the wheel. She finished the length of wool she had in her hand before leaping lightly to her feet, and taking my two great paws in her warm hands, she led me to a comfortable form and bade me be seated. Confound the women! I cannot make them out at all. The little wench, cock-a-hoop, and her lover imprisoned in the bowels of the earth. Egad, a fine look out for men if all women cared no more than a snap o' the finger whether their lovers or husbands were buried alive or buried dead. I had brought with me an arm-length of gay ribbon, but catch me giving it to this little callous! Then it crossed my mind that maybe she did not know; and thinking that some one less sympathetic might undertake to enlighten her, I made up my mind to do the job myself. But I had not got out of my mouth half a score of laboured words when she interrupted me with a peal of laughter, nodding her head the while to let me know that she knew all about it. Her laughter, however, ceased as suddenly as it had begun, and speaking vehemently, she said: "I translate, as is my wont, generously.

"Yes; they laugh now and look the one at the other mighty knowingly, and they wink and snigger, and the vixen she is puffed with pride. But wait. You shall see them on their knees. My lover is prepared for a longer stay than the father and Thorp can afford. All is well."

To hear this relieved my mind greatly. But the witch

seemed to look upon it in the light that everything which had been arranged to happen would happen. It never crossed her mind that there were such things as misfortunes in the whole world, or, we'll say, an accident. What if the maker of gods should fall ill of a fever, or fall over a rough rock and break his leg, or fall into the silent lake and get chilled to the bone, and no one able to get to him in his dismal prison! She did not dream of this as she again settled herself to the wheel, and I tried to bring myself to think a little the less of her for her thoughtlessness; but no! she was a comely lass, a graceful, dainty, hopeful, little lady, a trustful, buoyant, little Hebe. I drank the brew she gave me, and had not the heart to leave without giving her the bit ribbon I had placed in the crown of my cap for her. On the evening of this eventful day I at last learned the cause of the dispute between the Thorp and the maker of gods. As I have already explained, my experience in many lands has taught me that a sure way to cause people to grow suspicious, of one who is a guest among them, is for the stranger at the first to display a too curious interest in their circumstances and surroundings. Knowing this, I had carefully abstained from appearing to nose too deeply into this strange matter between Thorp and craftsman, while all the time, I need hardly say, I lost no opportunity to add further information to that already acquired. The good-wife, under whose hospitable roof I had stayed now for some days, with the ingenuity that is a virtue of woman alone, and assisted by the words I had been able to learn from my expatriated friend's vocabulary, managed to drive through my thick skull the better part of the pretty quarrel. I wondered if any packman but my own self could have been so stupid as to miss the meaning for so many days.

The good-wife had all along been an impartial spectator of the to-do. When I say of any woman that she is impartial it will, of course, be clear to all that she took no interest in the question one way or the other, for, of course, no woman can be impartial on any issue for longer than it takes to run three times round the town pump. Those anile nations, the Christians, use the figure of a woman to personify Justice. True, they have her eyes bound tightly about, her mouth shut, and have performed several other miracles with her, and put in her hands a pair of scales to relieve her somewhat of her independent judgment; but unless they have also her ears stopped and her feelings extracted, I can hardly see how they draw the jewel Impartiality from her. But it may be the female is a fit symbol of their justice. Well, my good hostess had all along fashed[1] her head but little over the matter, paying a strict and somewhat self-immolating attention to her household and her household gods, nosing after a speck of dust, flicking out a fly, polishing this utensil and that, mopping the floor, mending the clothes, and cooking in a way I vow no other woman in the land could cook. But the dramatic damming of the river at the behest of the termagant was an episode which no self-respecting housewife and mother could be expected to overlook; and mine hostess, her arms akimbo, waited to receive me when I returned from my visit to the lady of the wheel. She had heard the news, and with the promptitude of a reliant general, had taken a firm stand on one side of the quarrel. There is no need to tell which side she took, for a woman, who is a mother, her heart is big, and she invariably takes the side of the weaker in a quarrel, unless, of course, the quarrel be between an hereditary great one and a common born, when women, young or old, maiden or mother, will assuredly worship the title.

She began to me by saying that she would say nothing particularly good of the young man, for the gods knew he had his faults; nor would she say anything particular against the termagant, for it might be that the gods knew she had one or two virtues; but this she *would* say—and she said a great deal. She first began about the termagant, and miscalled her for a shrew and a vixen; she then piled mountain upon mountain of scorn upon the father and his silly old advisers, the patriarchs, and blamed them for allowing the vixen to get her finger in the pie; she said they had landed the ancient Thorp in as pretty a mess as town had ever found itself in, *that* they had; and that it would take cleverer men than ever the elders showed themselves to be to get the Thorp on its feet again, *that* it would; and she'd wager they found it easier to pitch the rock into the river than to set it up again, *that* she'd wager; and if they'd ask her she would tell them to their faces, one and all, that they were a precious parcel of idiots over the head of the whole business, and hear what they had to say for themselves.

I saw my opportunity, and stopping the good-wife her tongue, let her understand that for the life of me I could not make head or tail of the matter in dispute. This came as a great surprise to the good woman, and caused her to raise her eyebrows in astonishment; that anyone in the Thorp could be unacquainted with the cause of the stirring struggle had never crossed her mind. It took her from set of sun, through the gloaming, and until the men were quitting their benches for bed, to make me, dunce packman, understand. She first stood me up beside her, and stepping in front, assumed a solemn look, took a book in her hand, and commenced to mumble. This, it took me some time to make out, was the marriage-service. Then she forced me—was the maker of gods, I made out from her pointing to the mountain, and patting me on the shoulder—to shake my head in protest. Evidently I had no wish to marry. Next she braced herself up, threw back her head, and assumed the insipid look of the daughter of the termagant. O ho! I was expected to marry the daughter, and I'd see myself farther before I did. Then she sat down, and shaking her head as a maiden does whose hair hangs loose, she pretended to spin. The lady of the wheel! She caused me to smile and come to her side, and put my arm around her waist—thank all the gods and fates together her good man did not see me—and I knew I was making love to the black-haired wench. That seemed satisfactory. Then she flew into a violent temper, and stamped around—the termagant. But there! enough of this detail and of her actions. They were made necessary by the maker of gods, the young rascal, having omitted from the vocabulary he gave to me all words relating to love and marriage. The whole secret of the affair seemed to be that the termagant wished the maker of gods to marry her daughter, and the young man absolutely refused to do any such thing, but, instead, set his heart on one, the loveliest in all the Thorp, the spinner of fine wools, the weaver of tapestries, the witch of the raven locks. But, to be sure, it is necessary to have a license to marry, and this the termagant defied the father to give; and the father did not dare to disobey the shrew. I asked the good woman what of the town's property the maker of gods had taken with him into the mountain; but she smiled and led me to understand that she had no intention of robbing the plot of all its mystery for me, and so I dropped the matter, thinking it better not to be over-curious in my dealings with a woman. These revelations made the situation much clearer to me, although the why and wherefore of the Thorp's great anxiety to get the renegade to return was still unknown. However, if I must wait, wait I must. The key sentence I now knew read: "If you give me my marriage permit, I will give you your breeches." To discover the meaning of the latter part must be my object, and to come by it without appearing too curious.

## CHAPTER 9

The next morning, when the net was visited, no message from the missing one had been caught in its meshes. Search parties were therefore organized, and at the foot of the fall one made a discovery that caused a mighty sensation in the Thorp. It proved to be nothing more or less than one of the red boxes which had been sent to the maker of gods by the council of elders, and the box had not been opened. The finders of this looked upon the matter as ominous, indeed, and hurried with the box to place it into the hands of the father. When it came to be opened, lo! it was found to contain the Thorp's most important message to the young craftsman, the message that threatened harsh measures should he not return to the Thorp at once. Through some accident he had missed the missive. By unlucky chance it must have floated across the lake, and, catching in the current, passed through to the exit channel before the young man's quick eye had marked its progress on the bosom of the silent sea. Scarcely had the consternation born of this discovery reached its height, for they were a fair minded people, when in from above the falls came a goatherd with a message from the man in the mountain. This was opened in a great fluster of excitement, and at once read to the people. It proved to be a strange epistle indeed, scribbled in pencil on the back of an old parchment, which had evidently been folded in the young man's pocket for many days. He wrote, that having gone on an exploring expedition of some duration up the side of the crater, he found on his return that the surface of the lake had risen so as to flood the ledge of lava on which his tent was pitched, and that all his goods and clothing, edibles, firewood, and bedding had been washed into the bottomless well. He found himself, therefore, without shelter, without fire, without food, and as the temperature of the interior of the mountain was well known to many of them, they would realize, without words from him, in what a predicament he was now, from double starvation. He could not say whether or no this state of things had been caused by any action on the part of the people of the Thorp; but if it was of their doing, the Thorp must now be in the happy position of being able to congratulate itself on the complete success of the scheme; for a few days, under the best circumstances which he could hope to secure, would see the end of him in that icy hole. He would ask for no quarter. Indeed, should the Thorp attempt to send him supplies, there were a thousand chances to one against him being able to come by them, for the flood had carried away his canoe, and, as the water in the interior of the mountain was nothing more or less than liquid ice, it meant death to anyone who would venture into it. To finish, he said that maybe some of them thought that by thus putting his life in jeopardy he would be induced to cry "Mercy!" If such was the case, be begged to inform one and all that his safety or danger had nothing to do with the justice of his cause. Right was right whether he starved to death or no, and he would hold to his course come what might.

In this part of the world we know well that beasts, for instance, wolves, hunting in packs, and all eager to run down and secure the game which, without the assistance of his companions, no one of them could hope to bring to earth, will, nevertheless, in an instant turn round upon one of the pack which happens to receive an injury, and instead of helping the poor brute to the game, rend and devour him that in health was one with them all. To these examples we animals, who are accursed with the gift of being able to put our perverse moralizings to paper, point, and flatter ourselves on the score of our moral superiority to all other creatures of the earth. But, verily, we have no reason to plume ourselves so. The man we one day lift to our shoulders and carry before an admiring world is the next day cast to the ground and torn to pieces. The greater we honour, the more fiercely we revenge, when his feet are placed once more in the dust. And now an example of the truth of this was forthcoming. Yesterday the termagant had led the admiring mob. To-day—well, the ablest of women lacks the tact of perceiving when it is well to hold her tongue, and to keep out of sight, and, perceiving, to act accordingly. Diplomacy of the highest kind is a male attribute, for women are too single-hearted for fine duplicity.

When the sensations caused by the finding of the two

missives were buzzing in everyone's brain, the termagant, who up to this time had kept well in the background, thinking to check the rising tide of anger, stepped to the front, and essayed to address the people. It turned out to be an indiscreet and sorrowful appearance for her. Mine hostess, being a new recruit to the dispute, had, as new-comers will, worked her way to the front, and the moment she clapped eyes on the termagant she, honest woman, began such a tongue-lashing as only a plain spoken woman can give. The knowledge, unvoiced but intuitional, that the sympathies of those surrounding were with her, gave to her tongue the spice and gall that it might otherwise have lacked, as she shook one hard, red fist under the termagant's nose, while, with the other hand open and fingers spread apart, she protested to the crowd against the she-dragon and all her ways.

And the Amazon! Did she quail? Not a bit of it. Her face fell into a cruel set, her bosom heaved, and her dark eye flashed as she majestically confronted my hostess by stepping into the street. It was a foolish move on her part, for stepping from the dignity of the father's doorstep to the plebeian cobbles of the common thoroughfare reduced her to the level of a citizen, and with a burst of fury the crowd was upon her and had her overpowered—albeit, she scratched like a tigress. It was the women who seized her, and led by my amiable hostess they carried her where stood my humble ass tethered, ready for the pack. On the poor brute they placed the female tyrant, and a half dozen women holding her in place, the whole crowd—men, women and children—laughing hysterically and skipping around, marched to the river. I followed, fearing injury to the donkey. But no injury befell the beast. When the people reached the river the women took the termagant in their arms, unheeding the scratches and hair-pullings; and with as little to do as if they had been handling a bag of sand, they waded into the stream with their captive and dipped her under the running waters, it must have been half a dozen times, although to tell the truth I could not look on to count the exact number, for I do hate to see a woman tyrant or tolerant—any woman—brutalized. When they had satisfied their vengeance, and when the termagant was as limp as she had formerly been defiant, they took her out and placed her, dripping wet, on the back of my beast, and set her down at her own door.

It is a useful institution the ducking-stool. In this instance it gave to the people an opportunity to reduce the pride and intolerance of one who henceforth must be spoken of as the quondam termagant, and at the same time of easing their consciences of the full onus of the deed they themselves had done in pitching the boulder into the river. People are given to repenting of an injury to one person by injuring another. But as to this dipping I was not altogether ill-pleased, for the woman had laid violent hands upon me on the first occasion of our meeting face to face.

This burst of passion over, the atmosphere was cleared for the serious work that lay ahead of the Thorp. There could be no mistaking what the people intended to do. The late termagant and her brainless daughter must stand aside. The maker of gods must be released and restored to his place in the community, and his love troubles no longer interfered with. He must have his license and his liberty. So shouted the crowd, and so understood the father—glad to have the matter done with, I could see—and the elders, who also did not look at all ill-pleased either. The Thorp at once took on a wonderfully throng look. The workmen, who hitherto had worked at the triumphal arch in a listless, lackadaisical way, now swarmed along the scaffolding and set up a merry hammering, shouting to each other to buckle to with a will; while the carpenters alone excepted, all the men folk of the Thorp, under the leadership of the little, wizened, virile shoemaker, made off for the falls, the mighty blacksmith, with his sledge-hammer slung over his shoulder, forming the apex of the phalanx. Even as I was busy wiping my donkey dry after her dripping load, I heard the high, sharp click of a heavy hammer falling on hard stone.

Now as the Thorp was empty of men, and well-nigh so of women, and as the people had reached such a state of enthusiasm that my questionings, I felt convinced, would not appear out of place, I resolved to join the builders of the arch and give them a hand in a quiet way—for violent exertion is not for the good of a packman—to see whether I could not draw one of them into conversation. In this fortune favoured me, for a man, who as he worked cast many glances at the sun to mark its progress, took kindly to my inquiries, and as often as the overseer happened to be called to another part of the skeleton-like erection, he was graciously pleased to sit by me. No, the arch was not being builded in honor of the anticipated return of the maker of gods. A great man, the governor of this part of the world, was expected to visit the Thorp; a visit he paid to the place but once every five years, on purpose to receive from the father and elders an assurance of loyalty towards his person and certain dues in cash and kind, without which governors care little for verbal protestations of fidelity. The arch was in honour of this great man, although, my kind informant said, the people of the Thorp considered they were assessed too high in proportion to the amount of their loyalty. But this was not all. The better half of the row between my young friend in the mountain and the town turned out to be in regard to this same visit.

Yes, breeches were the causes of all the heart-burnings. It seemed that the official breeches which the town authorities were bound to wear on the occasion of the ceremony were fashioned out of chamois leather, after a peculiar and ancient cut, and around the knees, where indeed all badges of office should be—for office shackles a man morally and physically—were the chains of the town's authority made of beaten gold. Now it appeared that these indispensable articles of clothing had been passed into the care of the maker of gods to furbish and to burnish, and he, the young scapegrace, knowing well that the elders must have their breeches, made off with them into the mountain to hold them as hostages. Were it not for this, he could have stayed on the shores of Yellow Lake till the crack of doom for all the elders would have cared. But deprived of their state clothes, and the day appointed for the visit of the great one drawing near, no wonder the people began to pull long faces. The Thorp was being taught a lesson sore in the learning, to wit, it is not the rank that confers dignity on a man, but the clothes which the rank enables him to wear. The man is of no importance, the gear all important.

When I surveyed the events of the past few days, the gods give my donkey wings if it was not much like to one who at the end of the second act casts his mind back to the beginning of a play so that he may the better grasp the continuity and the whole. The determined lover, the equally determined termagant, the jejune daughter, the black-haired witch of the wheel, the henpecked father who refused the license to marry, the making away with the breeches, the outlandish hiding-place, the strange negotiations, the clever trap, the excellent ducking—I vow it was for all the world like to a tale told in the tent of the Bedouin, when the silver moon peeps over the rim of the desert.

The garrulous carpenter gone reluctantly to work I happened to glance up. There the great mountain looked down on the village with all its bustle and worry, and I aver the mountain seemed to smile at the tiny comedy.

# CHAPTER 10

But comedy has a way of changing at the most unexpected moment to tragedy. Even as I sat there listening to the carpenter, news came to the Thorp that those who had gone to the rock found themselves baffled in their attempts to remove the obstruction, and they now asked that the carpenters should join with them in the work, bringing timbers from the village yard for the purpose of prises. Oxen from the valley were being hurried forward, the long chains clanking from their yokes as the great-eyed beasts swayed from side to side in their haste. Trusting that by some lucky accident at least one of them would be washed within reach of the prisoner, the elders had sent a half score messages into the mountain, bearing words of comfort and cheer; that the obstruction to the stream was being removed as speedily as could be, that a canoe with food and clothing had been sent as far into the mountain as the water permitted, and that those in charge of the craft would put forward at the earliest moment they found a passage to be practicable. The man and the breeches could not be forthcoming a moment too soon to suit the Thorp, for the great man was timed to arrive on the next afternoon.

With the builders of the arch I made my way to the waterfall that now roared in good earnest over the boulder. And there saw I a scene which I still think of as one of the most pathetic of my long life of sight-seeing. The strong men had first attempted to break away the bank of the stream, but this they found to be quite impossible. The sides of the water-way were of solid rock, and to cut a channel through one or other of them must prove to be the work not of hours, but of many moons. So now every man had a different plan, and each was pursuing his own device. Some were preparing places for the timber levers in readiness for the arrival of the carpenters and oxen, others were prospecting the banks in the direction of the mountain, hoping to find a fissure in the rock which might be used to divert the course of the stream; and the blacksmith, his head and his great arms bare, the perspiration running down his face and falling in a stream from his smooth chin, he, having chosen a corner of the boulder which topped the running waters, swung his sledgehammer around his head and brought it down ring, ring, ring, ever on the same place. (For it is the nature of a stone, as it is of man, that it appears at its firmest when on the point of relinquishing the strife and rending asunder.) Already the great hammer was blunted to the likeness of an open sun-flower, and the face of the rock was dulled and bruised where the blows fell. But as yet there were no signs of any such result as the blacksmith hoped for. A good general as carefully plans for a retreat as for an advance. But in tipping this huge obstacle into the bed of the stream, the people had not given a thought to the getting of it out again. Whether or no they would have been able to remove the obstacle, had there been no deep body of running water to hinder them, I am sure I cannot tell; but this was clear, that under the present conditions there was little chance of their success. I realized this, and sorrow fell upon my heart.

Poor, headstrong, puny, proud young man in the mountain! We all saw that he would have to wait a longer time for the succour he so sorely needed than his body was likely to harbour his soul. No doubt by this time he had sat him down by the shore of the silent sea and modeled for himself, out of the clay picked from between the rocks, the little, peaceful god of eternal sleep. He would do this I knew before the chill and damp struck into his heart, to filch from him the gifts the gods had so freely given to him. How pleasant to know that he could make for himself his own god to comfort him when his eyelids were fluttering, like the wings of a stricken bird, to close forever. And poor, little bright-eyed lass, the wheel would not sing its droning song to-night, and the little cabin would be lonely and dark. Toward the hour of sundown the elders were called together, and from this time on till the morning light, sent at periods, certain suggestions to the workers, none of which proved of any practical value. When darkness fell, torches were lighted, and the whole Thorp turned out to lend a hand, or to look on. Indeed it was a weird sight. Torches spluttered and flared, men shouted, oxen strained at the chains, the falls growled angrily over the rock, the herculean blacksmith, seeming to gain strength as the hours flew, swung his great hammer; and above all, the mountain, looming out of the blackness and towering among the stars.

It must have been about the middle of night when we all heard a peculiar crash, and those of us near to the blacksmith saw the sledgehammer fly into a score of pieces; the hammer that was to shatter the rock, shattered in its endeavours. But although the tool was riven, the blacksmith still swung the handle around his head as he had done for many hours, and brought the end of it down on the self-same spot, until one standing near, touched him on the shoulder to tell him of the disaster. When the man's fingers fell upon his shoulder the blacksmith sprang as one stricken to the heart, and falling with a great splash into the stream would have been carried away by the waters had there not been ample assistance at hand. When it was seen that the blacksmith had given up the struggle and lay motionless on the bank, the hope that buoyed many of those who worked took flight, for they had all set their faith on his strong arms and heavy hammer. The ring of the broken hammer to every one of our ears sounded the knell of the exile in the mountain.

Morning came, bright and balmy, but the rays of the sun, as they struck upon the sullen rock, only showed more clearly the hopelessness of the situation. And as the sun shone full in the heavens, the last ox was unyoked, and the last workers marched wearily to the Thorp.

A community is one person multiplied an uncertain number of times. When a crisis comes in the affairs of a people, when a black-pinioned disaster is hovering over the community, the people are given to flying for help and protection to the one of themselves, whom, at the beginning of the civic year, they invested with chimerical power. From the date of such investment to the end of the term, they look upon the one of themselves, in whose hands are the seals of office, as though he were endowed with special powers from the gods. And the one of themselves himself is apt to fall into the same way of thinking. So the matter stands until the gods take it into their heads to smite the community. Then the people turn to their one in authority and see that he is but one of themselves; and he, poor soul! turns to the people and bewails the day he hearkened unto the flatterers, and upbraids them for giving him worthless power, and there is no help forthcoming. So it came about this day.

The men, the women, and the children, many of them weary to falling from their struggles with the obstinate rock, which like a deed done in anger could never be undone, still looked for help, and gathering around the door of the house of the father, they waited patiently to be spoken to and comforted. The elders still sat in council, if council it could be called where no one spoke, and each gave himself up to gloomy forebodings for the future of the Thorp, and anguished thought for the fate of the young man in the mountain.

But something must be done. Recognizing the claims of the people, the father at length appeared surrounded, as was the custom in those parts, by the patriarchs, and their faces were the faces of men without hope. At the sight of the old man a murmur of sorrow ran through the crowd, and many an apron was raised to tearful eyes, and I saw the backs of not a few grimy hands drawn sharply across downcast faces. All hope of rescuing the prisoner, and all hope of saving the reputation of the ancient and honourable Thorp had deserted the hearts of the people. I looked about me, but the little lady of the wheel was nowhere to be seen.

The father raised his two hands above his white head preparing, as I took it, to address the people. However, before a word passed his lips, the clatter of a horse's hoof striking upon the cobble stones of the narrow street caused every one to look in the direction from which the sounds came. There, plainly visible in the morning sunlight, his coat a blaze of crimson and gold, a scimitar clanking against the flank of the beast, came riding a courier who blew a brazen, blaring fanfare from a trumpet, the sound of which was tossed like a shuttle-cock from window to window as he guided his foaming steed direct to the father's house. This gorgeously caparisoned creature reined his horse to a standstill at the edge of the crowd, and, paying a sublime unheed to us all, again caused the air to ring with the brassy sound; and when he had caught his breath, announced in a high and plaintive voice that his master, Lord of all the provinces on which the sun took pleasure in shining, the Prince of the Earth, etc., etc., would do the Thorp the high honour of riding within her gates at mid-day of this same day, to receive the homage and submission of the authorities and inhabitants thereof, all and sundry, and also the dues which he was graciously pleased to accept as a token of their firm loyalty; furthermore, that the authorities and people were to take heed that they received the Prince of the Earth in becoming manner, or they, their children, and their children's children would rue it to their dying day! Amen. And with a final flourish of the trumpet, he disappeared a flame of fire and gold down the street and away.

## CHAPTER 11

The father, good soul! had scarcely lowered his hands before they were once more thrown up in despair, and the faces of the elders grew even longer than they had formerly been. The people stood dumfoundered. Verily, the bright sun of the ancient Thorp had set and set for ever. No welcome, and the great one thundering at the gate!

Well, it was no longer a place for a thrifty packman, and I began quietly to edge my way out of the crowd so as to lay hold of my ass and pack, and get well around the mountain before the great one descended upon the Thorp. At the outskirts of the crowd I paused to gaze, as indeed were all the people, at the departing splendour of the herald. While standing thus, it chanced I heard a little fellow, who tugged at his mother's petticoats, call upon her to look and see the strange bundle the man was carrying. It is the nature of one in sorrow to pay lavish attention to the whims of children, and the poor woman, although her attention was fixed upon the departing red and gold as though she were fascinated by the brilliant colours, turned her head in the direction to which the chubby little finger pointed.

The next instant we were all electrified by a shrill scream. Whirling sharply round, I was only in time to save the woman from falling heavily to the earth. As she swooned, her arm stiffened and her finger pointed. And there, as the gods shall feather my donkey, we saw within half a stone's throw of us all, and coming swinging towards us, the maker of gods himself. On one arm leaned the little lady of the wheel, cock-a-hoop as ever; and on the other, piled one on top of its neighbour, were the Thorp's official breeches, burnished and shining. I hope never again to pass through such an uncomfortable time. Our arms were full of women fainting, or, worse still, in hysterics, while children hung to their mother's skirts and bawled at the top of their voices, and the very men of us shouting excitedly to no one in particular, as if every soul of us had been struck daft by the sight of a ghost. Straight through the thick of us the young man shouldered his way, and striding up to the father and flinging the breeches on the bench before the door, he demanded :

"My marriage license, if you please. I return the breeches."

The old man stumbled back a couple of steps, and I verily believe would have fallen but for the press of elders at his back. At last be managed to gasp :

"You back!"

"My marriage license, if you please."

"But how did you get out of the mountain?"

"I was not in the mountain."

"Then in the name of all the gods, where were you?"

"Where a craftsman should be; in my workshop, exercising my brain to the glory of my native Thorp."

"In your workshop?"

"And would have been there still,—there for all eternity had it not been that the reputation of my beloved Thorp was in danger. As between his own wishes and his Thorp's credit an artist cleaves to his Thorp, for he alone of all those who live make it presentable to the world and guard its good name. Much would I have preferred to have remained in my workshop, but my Thorp cried, and-my marriage permit, if you please."

"You pretended"—began the old man, when the young man cut him short.

"Pretended? not a bit of it, I *was* in the mountain—in imagination, which is as real to an artist as to be in person in the mountain. I had to go to the mountain to bring you to your senses. I could not afford the time to take my hands from my work, so I stayed in my shop and sent part of my imagination to the Yellow Lake. An ounce of imagination is worth a ton of matter, as I hope this Thorp has now found out. My marriage permit, if you please."

We looked at one another. The father scratched his head, and a droll grin overspread his fat face as he said slowly : "It is already made out, and, believe me, young man, you may have a dozen of them for the asking."

"One's enough, although it has been so easily come by. Now if you patriarchs will assume dignity by getting into the Thorp's robes I will read to you the address of welcome I have embossed for the governor, and we'll be able to pack him away from the Thorp long before the gloaming. I have a little ceremony of my own to be performed before the sun sets tonight. On with your breeches."

Such a scurrying I never before had seen. The patriarchs were into their breeches before we of the crowd had ceased to gaze at one another, and I saw, as in a dream, the pompous, glorious prince ride in, and heard him, when he had got his hands on the gold, mouth a hollow, little address, which the people took for what it was worth; and later I attended with every soul in the Thorp who could leap or crawl—for the great drum called the people—the wedding of the maker of gods and the little lady of the wheel. The late termagant was there, a new woman, and her daughter fulvous and respectable as ever; my good hostess victorious; the blacksmith with a new sledge over his shoulder—everyone, in fact. And all seemed happy. The two were married under the triumphal arch, the name of the prince having been hastily removed the moment his fat back was turned-it is the way people have with their princes —and emblems of real joy and love hung in its place; and the people-I and my donkey at the head of them—escorted the happy pair to their house, and cheered them as they passed through the doorway. Then we sat down to think.

That evening, I fear I took quite as much good brew into me as the gods had ever intended I should in two hard sittings. We could do nothing but talk of the craft of the man. It beat anything I had ever met with. And when we thought the matter over, his being safe and sound in his shop explained many things, not the least of which was the cheerfulness of the little witch all the time her lover was supposed to be buried in the mountain. To be sure, it was all very plain now. She had easily learned the purport of each message which was being sent into the mountain, and at once let her lover know its essence, so that he might write the reply and drop it into the stream above the net during the hours of darkness; very likely this part of the job she also did for him.

After the first burst of joy over the recovery of the man and the breeches had somewhat subsided, and when they had drank a little more than enough, it was then that there stole into the breasts of the people a feeling of soreness, and a tendency to let the matter of the dispute pass for the time into sudden oblivion. For people do resent being tricked, especially if their neighbours know that they have been tricked-ay, even although those same neighbours have been hoaxed in the same way and at the same time. And when we came to thrash the matter out, as we did on the evening of the marriage, we could not congratulate each other on our sagacity. There was at least one event which might assuredly have caused us to smell a rat, if anyone of us had but kept a reasonably cool head on his shoulders. I refer to the red box which we had found shortly before the ducking of the termagant, the box which contained the Thorp's ultimatum to the man in the mountain. Had not an answer to the very message been received, an answer peculiarly scornful and defiant, from the young scamp? And yet the missive that called forth this reply had never been taken from the original box. It was as clear as day when we came to review the circumstances in the light of facts known. Truly we had been well fooled. Those two persons, the maker of gods and the little lady of the wheel, were just a whit too clever for everyday folk like their fellow-citizens, so thought the people of the Thorp. As the days passed, this feeling intensified into resentment against the two. Indeed, I could not wonder at such being the case, for every man and woman in the Thorp had been sorely tried, physically as well as in the spirit, over the matter; while all the time the only comfortable bodies in the place were the two who had the least right to be comfortable, to wit, the maker of gods, who quietly pursued his calling in his shop the while, and his hopeful little sweetheart, who kept him informed as to the Thorp's doings. Now this was a trifle too clever for ordinary plain folk, and cleverness never begets popularity in any country under the sun.

You may be sure I kept my eyes open, for I thought that I detected a tendency on the part of the people to hold me responsible, at least in a degree, for some part of the matter; it must have been because I was the last to speak with the culprit before his sham flitting to the shores of the Yellow Lake, and also that I franked the letter that caused all the commotion. Moreover, I was the only guest the two invited to sup with them after a mannerly length of time. As time passed, I saw the sulky animosity of the people growing more intense, and—a bad sign—the contempt of the maker of gods and his comfortable little spouse for their fellow Thorpmen and women increased as the resentment increased. Occasionally a red box would be seen to swim out of the mouth of the cavern and float gently down towards the hamlet. This would be quickly fished out, and without loss of time buried. But these boxes kept the sore open.

Having now well lined my pockets with gold, and filled my pack with nicknacks, which were cheap in the Thorp, I thought it high time to get away before a second dispute arose between the Thorp and her two eccentric citizens. So one fine morning—there had been ominous mutterings on the previous evening—I kissed the children and the hostess (she was a comfortable body and a sound cook, I believe she did not think unkindly of me, nor guess my age by half a score years or more), and bade my kind host "good-bye," and without further parley made off with my donkey and pack for parts unknown around the mountain, not at all ill-pleased to get so well away from the strange place. There had been rather too much material for wholesome speculation during my stay in the Thorp to suit even an artful packman. But as it was my custom never to let an occasion slip for improving my knowledge of human nature, I, at our first resting-place that day, made these observations to my cuddy, and as they seemed to meet with her approval, they are clearly good enough to give to the world. There are twelve in all. I would have liked to add another, something about the sad waste of time if one fashes his head about other people's goings-on; but although I am by no means superstitious, it has ever been my way to be careful, and to choose the safe side, and thirteen is held in Christian lands to be an unlucky number. So twelve it shall be:—

*A man's gods are of use to him-sometimes.*

*A huff often pays when it puts the sulky one to no inconvenience.*

*Our greatest strivings are after that which exists only in imagination.*

*Have a shrewd regard for superstition, but do not let it make you miss a meal.*

*If you dam a stream, look out for the overflow.*

*Do not judge a man by his breeches.*

*A clever deed brings its own retribution.*

*She can keep a cheery face who knows all is well.*

*Mountains, rocks, and floods are seldom found between true-loves.*

*He that journeys afar can tell a strange tale.*

*If you wish to find the man, find his wench.*

And most important of all:

*Pack, paunch, and pocket filled, fill the pipe,*
*and away.*

# NOTES

## CHAPTER 4

1. [sic] Chirrupy: lively, chatty

## CHAPTER 5

1. Expression of disparagement or contempt

## CHAPTER 7

1. (A neologism by the author) opposite of authenticity.

## CHAPTER 8

1. Scot: to trouble, inconvenience